EVERY WOMAN'S DREAM

By Lesléa Newman

Other Books by Lesléa Newman

Novels
Good Enough To Eat
In Every Laugh A Tear

Short Stories
A Letter To Harvey Milk
Secrets

Poetry
Just Looking For My Shoes
Love Me Like You Mean It
Sweet Dark Places

Non-fiction
SomeBODY To Love: A Guide to Loving The Body You Have
*Writing From The Heart: Inspiration and Exercises For Women
    Who Want To Write*

Anthologies
*Bubbe Meisehs by Shayneh Maidelehs: An Anthology of Poetry
    by Jewish Granddaughters About Our Grandmothers*
*Eating our Hearts Out : Personal Accounts of Women's Relationship
    To Food*

Young Adult Novels
Fat Chance

Children's Books
Heather Has Two Mommies
Gloria Goes To Gay Pride
Belinda's Bouquet
Saturday is Pattyday

EVERY WOMAN'S DREAM

SHORT FICTION BY
LESLÉA NEWMAN

New Victoria Publishers, Inc.

Published by New Victoria Publishers Inc., a feminist, literary, and cultural organization, PO Box 27, Norwich, VT 05055-0027.

Cover Painting by Yohah Ralph
Back Cover Photo by Mary Vazquez

Printed in the U.S.A.
1 2 3 4 5 1997 1996 1995 1994

                Library of Congress Cataloging -in-Publication Data
Newman, Lesléa.
    Every woman's dream : short fiction /by Lesléa Newman.
        p.   cm.
    ISBN 0-934678-62-6 $9.95
    1. Young women--United States--Fiction.   2. Lesbians--United States--
Fiction.   I. Title.
PS3564.E91628E94   1994
813' .54-- dc20   94-15390
                                                                CIP

Acknowledgements

For professional support, I am deeply grateful to my agent, Charlotte Raymond; and to the women of New Victoria Publishers: Claudia Lamperti, Beth Dingman, ReBecca Beguin and Deborah Dudley. In addition, I would like to thank all the small, independent women's presses and lesbian and gay presses I have been fortunate enough to work with; all the small, independent women's bookstores and lesbian and gay bookstores that have been kind enough to carry my books; and all the readers who have been generous enough to spend a few hours of their precious time immersed in my stories. In the words of Sandra Bernhard, "Without you, I'm nothing."

For their loving support and friendship, I thank Tzivia Gover, Jon Hirsch, Jess Wells, Judy O'Brien, Susan Waldman, Veda Andrus, Lynn Matteson, Marilyn Silberglied-Stewart, Tim Duffy, Janet Feld, Sue Tyler, and Faye and Bucky Wilson. And lastly, for everything and more, words cannot express my gratitude and love for Mary Grace Vazquez.

Credits

"All In A Day's Work" first appeared in *Common Lives/Lesbian Lives* Issue #39, Summer 1991.

"Comfort" first appeared in *Lesbian Love Stories, Volume Two,* edited by Irene Zahava, Crossing Press, Freedom, CA 1991.

"Every Woman's Dream" first appeared in *Word Of Mouth, Volume Two* edited by Irene Zahava, Crossing Press, Freedom, CA 1991.

"My Social Debut" first appeared in *Cachet,* preview edition, 1991.

"Memory" first appeared in *Quickies,* edited by Irene Zahava, Violet Ink Press, Ithaca, NY 1992.

"Of Balloons and Bubbles" first appeared in *Childless by Choice,* edited by Irene Reti, Herbooks, Santa Cruz, CA 1992.

"Still Life With Woman and Apple" first appeared in *Xanadu,* edited by Jane Yolen, TOR, New York, NY 1992.

"The AB Spot" first appeared in *Radical CHICk,* November, 1992.

"Let Me Explain" first appeared in *Art and Understanding,:The International Magazine of Literature and Art About AIDS,* Vol. 2, No. 1 Jan/Feb 1993; and *The Valley Optimist,* Northampton, MA April 12, 1993.

"Monday Night At The Movies" first appeared in *Woman In The Window,* edited by Pamela Pratt, STARbooks Press, Sarasota, FL 1993.

"Red, White and Absolutely Blue" first appeared in *Write From The Heart: Lesbians Healing From Heartache,* edited by Anita Pace, Baby Steps Press, Beaverton, OR 1991; and in *Eating Our Hearts Out,* edited by Lesléa Newman, Crossing Press, Freedom, CA 1993.

"What I Will Not Tell You" first appeared in *The Body of Love,* edited by Tee Corinne, Banned Books, Austin, TX 1993.

"How to Make Your Lover Miss You" first appeared in *How To,* edited by Irene Zahava, Violet Ink Press Ithaca, NY 1993.

"The Flirt" (in German translation) first appeared in *Mit Wurde und Feur,* edited by Karin Rick and Diana Voigt, Wiener Frauenverlag,1993.

"Less Ugly" first appeared in *Sportsdykes: Stories from On and Off the Field,* edited by Susan Fox Rogers, St. Martin's Press, 1994.

"With Anthony Gone" first appeared in *Art and Understanding: The International Magazine of Literature and Art About AIDS,* Vol. 3, No. 1, April 1994.

For Fern Silver and Peter Newman

in loving memory

—and for Susan—

CONTENTS

PART I: THE DEARNESS OF HER

My Social Debut

For the past three hours I'd raced around, making the zillion little decisions that had to be made: the red shirt or the black one, an undershirt or a bra, jeans or black chinos, an ear cuff or a gold loop, to mousse or not to mousse, that was the question. By the time Claudia picked me up at nine-thirty, I was exhausted.

"You look very handsome," she said, straightening my lavender tie (I had decided on the black shirt). "Ready to knock 'em dead?"

"Sure," I answered with false bravado.

"That's the spirit." Claudia slipped out my front door into the night with me at her high heels. "Who's driving?"

"You," I answered. "I'm too nervous."

"You'll be fine," Claudia said, unlocking the door of her Chevy Nova. "It's only a bar."

"A woman's bar," I corrected her.

"Of course a woman's bar." Claudia had been out for so long she just assumed when anyone said *bar* they meant a woman's bar or a gay bar. I, on the other hand, was quite new at all this. So new in fact, that this was my maiden voyage to Aphrodite's, even though it was a mere five miles from my apartment. "Listen, we're going to have a great time," Claudia chattered as she drove. "We'll have a drink or two, do a little girl watching, dance a few numbers...."

"Dance?" I gasped, holding my seat belt out a little so it wouldn't wrinkle my pants. "I don't know about dancing."

"C'mon, now." Claudia turned right. "You'll do fine." I took in a deep breath, as if inhaling her words would help me believe them.

What a predicament I was in: twenty-six years old and going through adolescence all over again. I felt so damn graceless, like I had all the social skills of a fried eggplant. Thank God for Claudia though. We'd been friends for years, and when I finally decided I was a dyke she didn't doubt me or kid me or even say, "I told you so." She took on my coming out as her pet project, a hobby of sorts. I didn't mind though; I needed all the help I could get. Claudia suggested all kinds of activities that would afford me the opportunity to meet women: pot lucks, support groups, ACT-UP meetings, but I'm a pretty shy person so none of that appealed to me. Now a bar on the other hand made sense; at least you don't have to sit in a circle, introduce yourself and tell everyone why you're there.

Claudia pulled into the parking lot, cut the engine and jumped out of the car. I lingered for a minute, twisting her rearview mirror toward me for a final inspection of my hair. "C'mon." Claudia yanked open my door.

"Okay, okay." I got out and looked at her turquoise blouse and black slacks. "Maybe I'm overdressed."

"Will you come on?" Claudia hooked her arm through mine and dragged me to the entrance. We paid our way in and made tracks over to a little table. Aphrodite's was your basic dive: a bar, loud music and a dance floor about as big as my kitchen table. "I'll get us some drinks." Claudia stood up as quickly as she'd sat down. "You want a beer?"

"Sure," I answered, pretending it was okay to leave me alone even for a split second. I was positive everyone in the place knew I was a first-timer. I looked around casually (I hoped) at the women playing pool, the women at the bar and the couples on the dance floor. A woman two tables over smiled at me as I caught her eye. I bared my teeth at her and quickly looked away as Claudia returned to our table. "Here." Claudia sat down across from me and handed me a bottle of Budweiser, which I immediately gulped.

"How's it going?"

"Okay, I guess."

Claudia leaned back in her chair to check out the crowd, stirring her wine spritzer with a straw. "Hey," she leaned forward, resting her elbows on the table. "Don't look now, but that woman over there is staring at you."

"Where?" I whirled around immediately, and knocked my beer over with my elbow. Claudia jumped up. "Subtle, very subtle," she said, righting the bottle. The damage was minimal, and we sopped it up with our napkins.

"Can we please go home now?" I pleaded as Claudia sat down again.

"No. Here," she said, holding out a cigarette. "To calm your gay nerves."

"Thanks." I flicked my Bic and took a drag. "Is she still looking?"

"As a matter of fact, she is."

"Oh, great." I tilted my head back and blew a perfect smoke ring into the air, hoping that would impress her so much she'd overlook my display of clumsiness. "What does she look like?"

"Oh pretty, very pretty." Claudia moved her eyes beyond my face and back again. "About your age. Blonde, and very stacked."

"You pig." I shook my head. "Rats. She's just my type." I bent down to untie and retie my Reebok, hoping to get a better look at her. But all I could see from this angle was a pair of jeans cuffed very nicely over two red flats next to a pile of spilled popcorn.

"Why don't you go over and say hi?" Claudia asked, nudging me with her elbow.

"Just like that?"

"Sure. What have you got to lose?"

I shrugged and took another drag on my cigarette before putting it out. "Oh nothing much. Just my pride, my dignity, my self-respect. My nerve." I stared past Claudia at the couples on the dance floor, doing their thing under the strobe light. Oh, to be up there belly to belly with some soft woman, my cheek resting against her hair....

"Earth to Iris, earth to Iris." Claudia waved her hand in front of my face and I reluctantly turned to her, thus interrupting my vicarious thrills.

"What?"

"Complications have set in. Prepare for Plan B."

"What happened?"

"Don't look now," Claudia grabbed my chin with both hands, as my head had already started to swivel, "but our heroine has just been joined by a companion."

"Oh no," I groaned, and then eager to show off my new vocabulary added, "Butch or femme?"

"Hard to tell." Claudia shifted her eyes without moving her head. "She's got that T-shirt, topsider, L.L. Bean look. Maybe she's a jock."

I groaned again. "They're probably girlfriends."

"Not necessarily." Claudia picked up her wine glass and took a delicate sip. "Number one, they're not touching anywhere. And B, she's still looking this a-way. As a matter of fact, she just pointed you out to her buddy."

"Really?" I ran my fingers through my brand new buzz cut, a gesture that makes me look exceedingly cool, if I do say so myself. "All right, Commander. What do we do?"

"Let me think a minute." Claudia tapped a polished fingernail against her cheek. "You could wander over to the bathroom and say hi when you pass her table."

"Claudia." I raised one eyebrow (another cool-looking gesture). "The bathroom's over there," I pointed behind her, "and she's sitting over there." I jerked my thumb in the opposite direction.

"So, who says the most direct line between two points is straight?" She looked at me with her head tilted to one side. "C'mon. Be brave."

I picked up my beer bottle and started rolling it between my sweaty palms. "I don't know. I think I'm too old for this."

Claudia patted my hand. "You're never too old, darling. You're just a baby."

"Don't touch me!" I shrieked, pulling away as though I'd been burned. "She'll think we're involved," I whispered, my voice starting to panic.

"Calm down," Claudia stage-whispered back. "You baby dykes." She shook her head and tapped her finger against her cheek again. "You could be really smooth and send a drink over to her table." She narrowed her eyes and peered through the semi-darkness. "Looks like she's got something creamy over there. A White Russian maybe, or a Brandy Alexander."

"Do people still do that?" I turned my head boldly to the side. The woman flicked a strand of her short blonde hair out of her eyes, smiled at me for half a second and then quickly started talking to her friend, their heads bent low over the table.

"Claudia, she's so cute," I whispered, even though there was no way she could have possibly heard me over the music. "And she smiled at me. I'm sure of it. What should I do?" I clutched Claudia's arm to keep from passing out in a dead faint.

"Hands off the merchandise." Claudia flicked my hand away as though it was a fly. "All right." She planted her palms firmly on the table and stood up. "It's time for action."

"What are you going to do?" I looked up at her nervously, for Claudia was capable of doing anything.

"I'm going to ask her friend to dance, even though she's hardly my type." Claudia rolled her eyes. "The rest is up to you." And before I could stop her, Claudia was over at their table with a big smile on her face, holding out her hand.

Swell, I thought, lighting up another cigarette from the pack Claudia had left on the table. Sure, go on, leave me all alone to make a fool of myself at my own social debut. I swiveled around in my chair to keep one eye on the dance floor and one eye on HER. She was watching the dancers, too, and I seized the opportunity to give her the once-over. She was young, I'd say twenty-two or twenty-three, and she was wearing a white tank top that looked great against her tan, with big white hoops in her ears. She turned toward me again and I quickly put out my cigarette, as an idea popped into my head. Before I lost what little nerve I had, I stood up, took a deep breath, and strolled over to her table.

"Hi, got a match?" I asked, gesturing with my half smoked cigarette.

"Yeah." She snapped open a red clutch lying on the table and handed me a book.

"Thanks." I relit my cigarette and put one foot up on the empty chair next to her, leaning my elbow on my knee. We watched the women on the dance floor for a while. Claudia bopped by, making a *c'mon already* gesture behind her partner's back.

"Some pretty good dancers out there, huh?" I asked. God, what a dumb thing to say. Especially since a slow song had just come on and the women out there weren't dancing so much as swaying to the music, locked together from shoulder to groin.

"Yeah." My tablemate sighed wistfully, laying one arm flat against the back of her chair and resting her chin on it.

We continued watching the dance floor like it was a made for TV movie. Claudia floated by, her chin resting on her partner's shoulder with a get-me out-of-here look in her eye.

"Um, do you like to dance?" I asked the back of my blonde beauty's head.

She lifted her chin and flashed me a perfect Pepsodent smile. "Yeah."

"Me, too." God, what an idiot. I took another puff of my cigarette and dropped it into an empty beer bottle on the table, as she turned back to our regularly scheduled program. Now the music was slowing down to a grinding, and I mean grinding halt. Pairs of women stood motionless, their arms wrapped around each other, smooching. Claudia is going to kill me, I thought, my eyeballs practically popping out of my head. But Claudia was nowhere to be seen.

I swallowed hard as I saw a woman in a leather jacket put her hand down her girlfriend's blouse. "Boy, there's some really great dancers out there," I mumbled to myself.

"Yeah." This time she didn't even turn around. Her shoulders rose and fell though, in a soft, sad sigh.

That did it. I popped a piece of Juicy Fruit into my mouth, cleared my throat, and uttered the two most difficult words to pronounce in the entire English language: "Wanna dance?"

"Yeah!" She turned around, looking so happy and excited that my stomach dropped to my knees. I led her out to the dance floor, worming my way through the various couples who stood stock still, like they were playing freeze tag. We looked at each other shyly for a minute, and then I opened my arms. She took a small step forward and just as I was about to gather her up like a bouquet of beautiful flowers, the music segued into a fast beat. Everyone started thrashing about wildly, while I stood there, my arms open, palms up to the sky like I was some jerk saying, "Hey, what do I know?" She moved into my embrace, held me tight and began leading me around the floor. We swayed together slowly, belly to belly, my cheek resting against her hair, and it was heaven, despite the occasional flailing elbows of the woman next to us that caught me once in the back and once in the side.

We moved past the bar where Claudia was sitting with my girl's friend. She pointed at me, made a circle with her thumb and forefinger, pointed at herself and then held her index finger straight up in the air. Translation: you-owe-me-one. I nodded and drifted happily away. When the third fast song came on, we broke apart and grinned at each other.

"I'm Iris," I said, holding out my hand.

"Annette." She shook my hand and held it tightly as we made our way back to her table where Claudia and Annette's friend were now sitting. We stopped a few feet away and turned toward each other.

"Is she..." we asked each other as if on cue.

"No," we both blurted out, and then burst out laughing. Relieved, hopeful, and scared shitless, I put my arm around Annette's shoulder and steered her to the table, praying I could get Claudia alone for a minute to ask her what in the world I was supposed to do next.

Memory

They say smoking pot affects your memory and I guess it's true because I really don't remember much about it and sixteen is way too young to be going senile.

I remember my best friend Pauline calling me up to invite me to sleep over and I remember lying to my mother and saying, "Of course Pauline's parents are going to be home," and I remember Pauline picking me up in her mother's car because she's a year and a half older than I am and already has her license.

I remember the first thing we did was smoke a joint and I remember asking Pauline if I could *lean* on her at least a million times and both of us cracking up every time I said it. I remember making the car window on my side go up and down with a little button on the door and thinking that was really cool and wishing my parents were rich like Pauline's, but she said she just wished her parents didn't go away so much because it was kind of scary to stay in that big house all by herself.

I remember then we got really hungry so we drove to Howard Johnson's for ice cream but I got a package of buttercrunch candies instead and I remember exactly what those buttercrunch candies tasted like: the chocolate part was all mushy so first my teeth sunk into them like mud and then I got to the hard buttercrunch part and when I cracked into it with my back molars, the crunch was really loud, like there was a car crash going on inside my mouth. I remember trying to explain all this to Pauline, but she was really into licking her ice cream cone around and around like a circle with no beginning and no end which she thought was just like life and terribly profound though I don't remember why. But I do remember that her ice cream was vanilla with just a few chocolate chips here and there which looked kind of like Pauline because she has this really white skin with a bunch of beauty marks all on one cheek.

Then I remember we drove back to her house and spent about an hour trying to figure out which key went into which lock and laughing so hard about it I got a bellyache which could have also been on account of the twelve buttercrunches jammed into my stomach but I don't think so. Then Pauline finally got the door open and all of a sudden this incredibly loud noise was shrieking through the entire neighborhood just like when you're standing under the bell at school and it goes off for a fire drill only eight hundred times louder, and Pauline had to run to the phone and call the police and explain that she had accidentally set off the burglar alarm and the secret password was spaghetti so could they please shut it off and not come arrest us for breaking into the house and being stoned.

After that we were kind of jumpy so we decided to take a bath to calm our nerves, because that's what our mothers do when they're nervous which is practically all the time. I remember Pauline filling the heart-shaped tub in her parents' bathroom with soap bubbles that smelled like flowers, and I remember thinking they were just like snowflakes with no two being exactly alike and then Pauline told me to look up and I saw a million me's on the ceiling which was full of tiny mirrors and I remember waving and a million me's waving back and that was really, really cool. Then Pauline started singing "Hey, Big Spender" just like that woman on the TV commercials for White Owl Cigars and stripping off her clothes and twirling them over her head and flinging them around like Gypsy Rose Lee. That really cracked us up. I was in the tub already and Pauline was stark naked when the doorbell rang. I remember she put on her father's blue terry cloth robe which was about twenty sizes too big for her and said HIS on the pocket besides and that made us hysterical for some reason and then the doorbell rang again so she went to get it.

A minute later Pauline came back with Gary, which I guess was all right, I mean he is my boyfriend and everything, but he could have called. So then I remember we smoked another joint with me in the bathtub covered with soap bubbles like a movie star and Pauline in her father's terry cloth robe and Gary just in his regular clothes, I guess. Then Pauline said she was going to sleep and then it was just me and Gary and I don't remember me getting out of the tub or him getting undressed but I must have and he must have because then we were up on Pauline's parents' big bed which had buttons that made part of the bed go up and part of the bed go down and part of the bed shake all over which was supposed to be sexy I guess, but actually made me kind of sick.

Then I remember Gary saying, "C'mere," which is what he says in the car when he wants to make out, so I said okay even though I didn't really feel like it, but he didn't take my hand and put it down there like he usually does. He laid down on top of me and moved around and grunted and I remember staring up at the ceiling which didn't have a million tiny mirrors on it like the bathroom but was totally white except for this little black dot that looked just like one of Pauline's beauty marks.

Then Gary rolled off me and kissed my cheek and went to sleep and I remember lying next to him with the room kind of spinning and all those buttercrunches in my belly kind of swimming, and this Peggy Lee song going round and round in my head, you know the one where she keeps asking: *Is that all there is? Is that all there is?* And I guess that is all there is because like I said, I think the dope's gone to my head because I really don't remember much. Funny how you remember all those crazy little things that don't mean anything like the sound of Pauline's laughter and her beauty marks and the way she licked her ice cream round and round, and then something really important happens like you lose your virginity which is supposed to be like this major event in your life that will only happen once and you don't even remember the tiniest little thing about it.

Water From A Stone

Your lover rings the doorbell. You stand beside her wishing you could touch her, but following instead, the unspoken rule. You wait for a long moment until the door opens. "This is my mother," your lover says. "This is my father."

"Nice to meet you," you say to your lover's mother. You nod at your lover's father. So you're the one who raped her when she was a baby, a little girl, a teenager, you want to say. I've heard so much about you. But of course you don't say that. Another unspoken, yet understood rule.

You follow your lover and your lover's parents into the kitchen for a lunch of cold cuts that taste like cardboard. No one says much, except your lover's mother who every now and then asks, "Would you like more potato salad?" Or, "How about some soda?"

Your lover's father disappears behind a section of the *Sunday Times*. How rude, you think, insulted, even though your lover has warned you about his lack of social skills. You take this golden opportunity to study him. He has thick black-framed glasses and a completely bald head, dotted with many freckles. You wonder what picture would appear if you played connect-the-dots on his scalp. He is quite ordinary. Extraordinarily so. You were expecting some sort of monster, but no, there he is, your basic man, lifting a coffee cup into the air to receive a steaming refill from his wife.

The sunlight streaming in through the window shines on top of his head like a spotlight searching for someone. You stare at it until he turns the page of his newspaper. Then you look away and then you look back. This time you notice his hands. They are small and delicate, like a woman's, almost. His fingernails are glossy, as though they have been buffed. Maybe even polished. This surprises you.

After lunch your lover's father retires to the den for a nap. You follow your lover and your lover's mother out into the backyard, each of you armed with a section of the newspaper. You sit on lounge chairs and read the paper, or pretend to. You are certainly not reading the paper and your lover hasn't read a newspaper in the year and a half you've known her. Ah, but your lover's mother is definitely reading the paper, parts of it out loud, in fact.

"Three teenagers in a little town in Ohio all killed themselves in the same week. Isn't that awful?" You nod, for she seems to be addressing you. "Oh, look. Macy's is having a sale on those cute sundresses. We could take a ride over if you're interested." She holds out the paper to your lover who does not respond. Your lover, you know for a fact, hasn't put on a skirt, let alone a dress in over ten years.

It is time to go. Your lover's mother gives you a bag of plums for the long ride home. Your lover's father rouses himself and stumbles out of the den to say goodbye, his glasses slightly askew. You get in the car and your lover's mother and father stand in the driveway, waving. You wave back, hating your lover's father in his striped polo shirt and plaid Bermuda shorts. You hate him, yet you feel a little sorry for him at the same time and this is something you do not like about yourself.

You pull of of the driveway and glance at your lover, sitting beside you with the bag of plums on her lap. "You okay, honey?" you ask.

"Fine," she says in a hollow voice. You know that voice. You look over at her again, seeing the same brown eyes you have looked into a thousand times, only this time there's no one behind them. You drive around the block and pull the car over to the side of the road. You take her in your arms, not caring who might walk by in this straight suburban neighborhood. You hold her. You tell her she is very brave. You tell her how much you love her. You call her secret pet names only the two of you know. You wait. You wait until her body no longer feels like a rock in your arms. You wait and wait. It takes a very long time. You are patient, for you have done this many times before, mostly but not always in bed when your lover wants you to touch her but then she grows afraid and her body turns to granite. You hold her, convinced you can coax water from a stone. You hold her and talk to her and stroke her hair and soothe her and tell her how brave she is and how strong she is until finally the tears come and her body melts into skin and blood and bone. You hold her right there in her old neighborhood until her tears are spent and she has come back fully into herself. And then you take her home.

Of Balloons and Bubbles

I am not a mother by choice, meaning I have chosen not to be a mother, as opposed to Maria, who is also not a mother by choice, meaning she is a mother though she did not intentionally choose the position. Maria merely fell in love with Stephanie, who three years down the road announced that she was going to have a child. And so she did.

Now it is two-and-a-half years since Frannie came into the world and Stephanie has had to take a part-time Saturday job in a music store to help pay for Frannie's day care. Which means Maria has to watch Frannie on Saturdays. And it's not that Maria doesn't love Frannie to pieces, you understand. It's just that having a child was never in her scheme of things and every once in a while Maria longs for a luxurious Saturday afternoon when she could practice her viola in peace (she and Stephanie met in a music theory class) or hang out with a friend downtown over a cup of cappuccino, or even go grocery shopping without her two-and-a-half year old angel taking every box of cereal off the bottom shelf to see what's inside.

And that's where I come in. You see, as my biological clock continues to tick away like that obnoxious stop watch on *60 Minutes,* I've been reconsidering my decision. Lately, every once in a while (I suspect when I have PMS) I experience a strange longing to hold a baby in my arms, to rock a child to sleep, to bake cookies and pour tall glasses of milk. Lately I've been wondering what my daughter would look like (she's always a daughter in my fantasies). Lately, visions of me sitting peacefully in a rocking chair with a cup of tea, my little bundle of joy blissfully asleep beside me, have been dancing through my head.

Usually when I am in this particular mood, I pop over to Maria and Stephanie's house and Frannie obliges me by sitting on my lap and hearing my latest rendition of *Green Eggs And Ham*. Today though my hormones must really be going wild, for I have spent the entire morning at Caldor's, not buying the plastic and window caulking I need to get my apartment ready for winter, but oohing and aahing and even shedding a tear or two over the tiniest, sweetest pair of black patent-leather Mary Janes you've ever seen. Then I went home and called Maria with a daring proposal: I offered to take Frannie off her hands for an entire Saturday afternoon. It's time for me to really try out this motherhood business once and for all, I told her. And she agreed.

It is a gloriously sunny, crisp, New England afternoon, the kind we Vermonters remember on sub-zero January days when we're wondering why in the world we live in this state. I am going to take Frannie to a farm stand to pick out a pumpkin and then we're off to the park for a rollicking afternoon on the swings. Or at least that's the plan. I arrive at one o'clock, as pre-arranged with Maria. "Hello," I call as I push open the door. "Anybody home?"

"Nomi! Nomi!" Frannie comes tearing into the front hallway wearing nothing but a yellow T-shirt that says GIRLS ARE GREAT on it. "Nomi!" she shrieks again, quite pleased with herself, as she has just learned to say my name two weeks ago.

"Hi, Frannie-pie. Ready to go?" A rhetorical question, as Frannie obviously can't go out in the October air, glorious as it may be, without her pants on. I squat down and give her a hug. "Where's Maria?"

"'ria! 'ria!" Frannie races through the living room which is scattered with building blocks, the colored rings of a stack toy, several picture books, a teddy bear and Frannie's bottle.

"Hi, Naomi." Maria emerges from the bedroom waving a pint-sized pair of panties. "Frannie, you ready to put these on, or do you want to try the potty again?"

"Potty." Frannie runs into the bedroom and disappears, presumably to perch her tiny cellulite-free bottom on the potty.

"Excuse us," Maria goes in after her. "We're running on baby time here."

"That's okay." One of my short-comings as a lesbian is always being on time, or worse yet, arriving early. I can see having a child would certainly cure me of that habit. "I'll just make myself at home," I call, flopping down on the couch, right on top of a graham cracker smeared with strawberry jelly.

I clean my jeans and sit down again, more carefully this time, just as Frannie gallops back into the living room, in her T-shirt and underwear. Progress is definitely being made. "Nomi, I pooped!" she announces, flopping down on the floor and picking up a block. "I build house."

"Frannie, here's your overalls, honey. Let's get dressed so you can go get a pumpkin with Naomi."

"Pumpkin! Pumpkin!" Frannie dances around the room with Maria following her, miniature overalls, socks, shoes and sweater in hand. I am dazzled by this constant motion. Finally Frannie is ready and Maria's face sags with relief.

"Why don't you just take my car?" Maria asks, grabbing her keys from a hook on the wall. "The stroller's in the trunk and the car seat's all set up." She hands me the keys and a huge blue bag. "There's a set of clothes in there, a bottle of apple juice, some books, her stuffed piggy, whatever. I think there's some toys in the car, too. I'll walk out with you." She turns to Frannie. "Ready?"

"Up." Frannie raises her arms and Maria picks her up, for her two-and-a-half year old legs aren't quite long enough to navigate the steep back steps yet.

We get to the car and Maria buckles Frannie into her car seat, tucking a bottle, a plastic set of car keys, an elephant puppet, a small Kermit the frog, and a Sears catalog around her, even though the farm stand is a mere five minutes away.

"Isn't she a little young to be thinking about washing machines?" I ask as Frannie immediately goes for the Sears book.

"She loves the pictures," Maria replies, putting the blue bag in next to Frannie. "There's a hat in there it case it gets windy, but I don't think you'll need it. Bye-bye Frannie-love. Here's a kiss." Maria gives Frannie a hug and a kiss and starts to back out of the car.

"Kiss Goofy," Frannie says, kicking her foot up and extending the plastic Goofy bow-biter on the edge of her shoelaces.

"Bye, Goofy. I'll blow him a kiss." Maria kisses her own palm and blows in Goofy's direction. "Here's one for Son of Goofy." She blows a kiss toward Frannie's other foot, straightens up and closes the car door. "Bye, you two. Have fun." Maria stands on the edge of the driveway while I start the car and shift into reverse.

"My painting hurts," Frannie calls from the back.

"What, sweetie?"

"My painting hurts."

"Your painting hurts?" What could that possibly mean? I put the car back into park and swivel around in my seat. Maria, smelling trouble, walks back to the car.

"Her painting hurts," I inform Maria.

"Your painting hurts?" she asks, opening the car door again.

"My painting hurts," Frannie repeats loudly, frustrated I imagine by the non-intellectual life forms she is dealing with here.

"Your painting hurts," Maria says to Frannie. "Show me where."

"Here." She points under her bottom and squirms in her seat.

"Let's see." Maria lifts Frannie to reveal a crumpled up piece of scratchy art work. "Did I put you down on your painting? Silly me. I'm sorry." She removes the painting and buckles Frannie in again. "There, that's better. Everything hunky-dory now?"

"Yeah." Frannie settles in and puts her bottle into her mouth.

"Bye." Maria waves as I back out of the driveway without incident. It is one-forty-five, according to the clock on the dashboard. Not bad, I suppose, for baby time.

"Look at the leaves, Frannie, aren't they pretty?" I say, pointing out the window.

"Yeah," Frannie answers, dropping her bottle. *Yeah* is her favorite word. "My bottle. My bottle, Nomi." I look in the rearview mirror to see her reaching for it, straining against her seatbelt.

"Hold on, Frannie, I'll get it." I reach behind my seat, keeping one hand on the wheel, feeling for the bottle with the other. Thank God Maria has an automatic, I think as my fingers brush the bottle, sending it further out of reach. I contemplate pulling over, but with a little twist I manage to retrieve Frannie's bottle and undo fifty-five dollars worth of chiropractic work at the same time. "Here you go, Ms. Frannie." I extend the bottle to her and make a wide right turn. Now we are on Route 57, a beautiful country road.

"We're almost at the pumpkin patch," I sing out, opening my window a little. "Ummm. Doesn't the fresh air feel good, Frannie?"

"Yeah," she says, this time both hands holding fast to her bottle.

"Here we are." I pull the car over to the side of the road where a long line of cars have parked. "Look at all those pumpkins, Frannie." I point out the window. Orange spheres everywhere, large and small, as far as the eye can see.

"Pumpkins! Pumpkins!" Frannie pushes at her seatbelt with both hands. "I want out. Out!"

"Just a second, honey." I get out of the car and walk around to the side away from the road to free Frannie. She's off like a shot, yelling, "Hi pumpkins! Hi pumpkins!" and waving her little hand with me trotting after her. The place is swarming with kids and adults, all buying pumpkins, gourds and gallons of apple cider.

"I can't." Frannie is pulling at the stem of a pumpkin twice her size, next to a sign that says DO NOT PICK UP PUMPKINS BY THEIR STEMS. "Nomi help. Nomi up."

"That pumpkin's a little too big, Frannie. Let's go look at the ones over there." I point to a large area of kid-size pumpkins and Frannie runs over with me at her heels.

"This one. This one." Frannie points excitedly at a huge orange plastic garbage bag with a jack-o-lantern face printed on it, stuffed to the gills with leaves. "I want this pumpkin." She flings her arms around it and tries to pick it up.

"That's not real." An older, and obviously more worldly little girl in a T-shirt that says CLASS OF 2001 speaks solemnly to Frannie. "That's not a real pumpkin," she repeats, this time to me.

"Well, thank you for pointing that out," I say, my voice just as serious. I squat down and pick up a fat little pumpkin. "How about this pumpkin?" I ask Frannie, holding it out to her.

"No."

"How about this one?" I offer another.

"No."

"Ooh, look at this one. See what a nice curvy stem it has?"

"No."

"All right." I'm no fool. This could go on all day. I straighten up, my knees cracking. "I guess we won't get any pumpkins, then," I say, sounding more than a little like my own mother.

"Pumpkins!" Frannie trots across the farmer's yard to an old- fashioned wagon filled with gourds. "Up," she says, lifting her arms to me.

I pick her up, praying that my chiropractor will have an opening this week, and point to the gourds. "See, Frannie, these are gourds. There's green ones, and yellow ones..." I pick one up to show her. "Sometimes there's seeds left inside and you can make a sound with them." I shake the gourd but nothing happens. No matter though, as Frannie is not in the least bit interested in my music lesson. "Pumpkin!" she yells, shattering my ear drum and squirming out of my arms. "My pumpkin. Mine." She reaches toward a small, round, orange gourd.

"That's not a pumpkin, honey. That's a gourd. It looks like a pumpkin though, doesn't it?" I grab it off the wagon and hold it up. "See, it's round like a pumpkin, and it's orange like a pumpkin..." I gesture toward the zillions of pumpkins surrounding us and Frannie snatches the gourd out of my hand.

"My pumpkin," she croons happily. "My pumpkin."

"But Frannie." I don't know what to say. Obviously the child is in love and who am I to spoil it for her? But then again, was I screwing her up for life by letting her believe something was what she wanted it to be, rather than what it really was?

"Okay. Let's go give the farmer a quarter." I put Frannie down and we walk over to a man in a plaid shirt and overalls, with a white cloth money bag tied around his waist. After all, she isn't hurting anyone with her little delusion, I reason with myself. And life is full of disappointments as it is.

We make our purchase, get back in the car and turn around to head for town, our destination being the school yard, also known as the park.

"Oh look, Frannie. A fair." I nod my head out the window toward the town common, where autumn festivities are in full swing. There's craft booths set up and a band and a big food tent. A banner stretched across the road proclaims: AUTUMN FESTIVAL, SATURDAY OCTOBER TWELFTH. "Want to check this out, Frannie?" I ask.

"I want a balloon," Frannie says, reaching toward a bunch of orange, yellow, and red balloons tied to a tree bordering the commons. "My balloon, my balloon," she calls as we drive by.

"One balloon for Ms. Frannie coming right up." I take a left turn and look for a place to park. The street is jammed and I finally find a space three blocks away.

"We'll have to take the stroller, Frannie-pie," I say, shutting the ignition. "This is a big walk." And I know for a fact my back cannot possibly withstand lugging an extra thirty-something pounds up this hill.

I leave her in the car while I open the trunk, take the stroller out and try to figure out how to uncollapse it. It somehow works on the accordion principle, I know, like those old-fashioned wooden drying racks, but I can't seem to get the sides straightened out and even. I'm working up quite a sweat here, so I take off my jean jacket and fling it into the back seat next to Frannie. "You're being so nice and patient," I say, giving Frannie, with that one remark, more positive reinforcement than I received in my entire childhood. "Just one more second and Aunt Naomi will get it together." I wrestle with the stroller again to no avail. Finally I see a man and a woman with a Frannie-size child in a similar contraption coming up the street. I swallow my butch pride and ask for help.

"Here." The man pushes a lever on the side of the wheel, snaps the stroller open and locks everything in place. "Just pull this to fold it up," he says, flicking the little lever.

"Thanks," I say. I was kind of hoping for the woman's assistance, as a good role model for Frannie, but oh well. Instead of fussing with the stroller, she walks over to the back of the car, pokes her head in and pokes it back out. "How old is she?"

"Two-and-a-half."

"What's her name?"

"Frannie."

"Hi Frannie. Are you going to the fair?" She reaches into the car and strokes Frannie's hand. "Oh, what nice soft skin you have. What a nice, soft hand." The woman straightens up and says to me, "God, remember when we had skin like that?"

We. Not only can I not remember my skin ever being butter-soft like Frannie's, but I also cannot remember the last time a straight woman lumped me together with herself into a collective pronoun. Maria says having a kid is like being let into this secret club; straight women talk to her all the time now. Until of course they hear Frannie call her "'ria" instead of Mommy, and ask her why, and Maria explains that she is Frannie's co-mother, her lover Stephanie is Frannie's birth mother. Then they usually just nod politely, and clutching their own child, hastily slink away.

"Let's go, honey." Father and son are impatient, though I sense Mom would be happy to stand around chatting all day.

"Bye-bye, Frannie." The woman waves and Frannie waves back.

"She looks just like you," she says, ambling away with her family. Strange, Maria says people say that to her all the time, too. I laugh and take it as a compliment as I duck into the car to remove Frannie. Before she can demand to walk, I buckle her into the stroller and we're off.

The fair is mostly local craftspeople selling patch-work quilts, stoneware pottery, wooden pull toys, crocheted booties and sweaters, and fresh honey along a narrow midway of tents and booths. There's a bluegrass band playing over by the food tent and three black dogs of various sizes, all with bandannas around their necks are frolicking in the grass. People mill about, looking at the crafts, eating hot dogs and generally enjoying what is undoubtedly one of our last truly warm days for at least six months. I crouch down to unbutton Frannie's cardigan, for in the sun it is almost hot.

"I want out. Out, Nomi," Frannie says. "My balloon."

"Okay, honey. Let's go find your balloon." I take her out and we walk along, pushing the empty stroller together. "There's the balloons," I say, pointing to the far end of the crafts aisle where a bouquet of balloons wave in the air. We make our way over to them, steering the stroller around people, dogs, tent poles and table legs.

"What color do you want, Frannie?" I ask, looking up at the bunch of balloons in the sky. "See, there's red, yellow, green, purple, blue..." I turn from the balloons toward Frannie, but she is no longer at my side. "Frannie? Frannie!" I turn around, my heart thumping wildly, my imagination already picturing her dear little face on the side of a red and white milk carton: FRANNIE MATTERAZZO-HARRIS, LAST SEEN OCTOBER TWELFTH...

"Frannie!" I yell again, relieved to spot her not ten feet away, her hands covering her ears. I desert the stroller and go to her. "What's the matter, honey?" I squat down, my knees cracking again. "Are you scared, sweetie-pie?"

"Yeah." She doesn't take her hands away from her ears.

"Are you afraid the balloon will make a big noise?" Maybe she'd accidentally popped a balloon once.

"No." Frannie shakes her head vigorously.

"What then, honey? Should we forget about the balloon?"

"My balloon." She reaches one hand out tentatively, then claps it back over her ear again as a woman with green frizzy hair and a big red nose comes over to us. She is wearing a pink and yellow checkered clown suit, with enormous purple sneakers on her feet.

"Hi there, little girl. Would you like a balloon from Emma the Clown?"

"No!" Frannie shrieks, puncturing my other ear drum. She collapses into a fit of sobs and I sit cross-legged on the grass, pulling her into my lap.

"Whoops. Sorry." The clown backs away toward her helium tank where a young customer is waiting.

"Are you scared of the clown, Frannie?" I ask, holding her tight.

"Yeah." She punctuates her answer with a howl I'm sure Maria hears back in their apartment. I rock Frannie on my lap, wiping her face gently with the end of my sleeve, since of course I don't have a tissue or a hanky on me. She continues to cry softly as I ponder the situation. I could say to her, *it's all right, Frannie, clowns are fun, they're not scary,* but that wouldn't help her trust her own instincts now, would it? So maybe it would be better to agree with her, and say, *yes Frannie, that's a very scary clown.* But would that make her even more fearful and ruin her chances of ever enjoying a trip to the circus or a parade? I sigh and stroke her fuzzy head. What's a mother to do? I decide to go the route of my own mother and sidestep the issue of Frannie's feelings in favor of offering a practical solution.

"You wait right here, Frannie, and I'll get you a balloon, okay? You sit here and I'll deal with the clown, all right?"

"Yeah."

"I'll be right over here by the balloons, see? I'm only three steps away, okay?"

"Okay." I ease her off my lap and hobble over to the balloons, as my right foot has fallen asleep. "What color do you want, honey?" I call.

"I want red."

"Okay. Stay right there." I keep an eye on her while the clown fills a red balloon with helium and ties it to a long white string.

"Here you go." Frannie takes the balloon's string from me. "Come, let's go to the park." I start pushing the stroller and she scoots under my arm.

"Frannie push," she says, holding onto the stroller. Immediately her balloon takes flight, soaring skyward toward balloon heaven.

"My balloon. Bye-bye balloon." Frannie waves, fascinated for an all-too-brief moment. Then her lower lip starts to tremble and her eyes fill.

"I'll get you another one," I say quickly. "Let's go back to the balloons." Again I leave her and the stroller three steps from the clown who is handing a green balloon to a little boy's mother. She takes it, ties a slip knot in the string and loops it around the little boy's wrist.

Oh, right, I think as I order another balloon. Of course you don't hand a helium balloon to a child. You attach it to them. Fortified with this new knowledge, I take the balloon to Frannie and tie it to her wrist. "All set?" I take a few steps with the stroller.

"Frannie push." She butts her head under my arm and takes over.

"Okay." We proceed until she crashes into the tent pole of a woman selling wind chimes and stained glass window ornaments. The collision creates quite a musical racket, but nothing breaks, thank God.

"Frannie, it's too crowded for you to push the stroller by yourself." I put my hand on the stroller, which she promptly pushes away. "Do you want to ride in the stroller?"

"No. Nomi ride. Frannie push."

"I'm too big to ride in the stroller, honey," though at this point, believe me, I do appreciate the offer.

"Balloon ride."

"You want your balloon to ride in the stroller?"

"Yeah."

"Okay." I slip the string off her wrist, secure it around the stroller and set the balloon in the stroller seat. "There, how's that?" I let go, and the balloon, being full of helium, bobs up, straining at its string.

"Balloon ride," Frannie insists, reaching up for it.

"Sweetie, the balloon can't ride. It's full of helium," I say, wondering what in the world that can possibly mean to a two-and-a-half year old child. "You want to hold the balloon again?"

"Yeah."

I untie the balloon from the stroller, and noticing Frannie's wrist is a little red, I tie the balloon to the strap of her overalls. A vision of Frannie floating up to the treetops like Winnie The Pooh crosses my mind, but she stays firmly rooted to the earth.

"How's that?" I ask. Frannie looks up. "Hi balloon," she sings out, waving. We push the stroller together and she doesn't move my hand away until we have taken five whole steps.

"Frannie, I have to help you push the stroller. It's too crowded here for you to do it by yourself."

Frannie lets out a wail. "No. Frannie push. Nomi go away."

I am cut to the quick. Rejected by a two-and-a-half-year old? "What's wrong, Frannie-pie?" I wonder if she's still a little flipped out over the clown. Maybe there's a load in her pants? Nope. Could she be hungry? "You want a hot dog, Frannie?" I ask, wiping her face with my sleeve again.

"Yeah," she sobs.

"Let's go then." Two more steps and again Frannie slaps my hand from the stroller.

"Frannie." My voice is firm, yet loving, I hope. "Here's your choice: you can either ride in the stroller or let me push it," I say, not giving her a choice at all, a handy trick I picked up from Maria. Frannie continues to scream and cry as I buckle her into the stroller, acting like the countless parents in supermarkets I have always glared at with disapproval.

We make our way over to the food tent, Frannie's balloon hitting me in the face with every other step. She continues to howl and I ignore the stares, real and imagined being thrown our way. I park her at the entrance to the food tent. "Hang on, honey, I'm right here. One hot dog coming up." As soon as I take two steps up to the table, Frannie quiets down.

"You want ketchup or mustard?" I say over my shoulder as a woman hands me a hot dog.

"Ketchup," Frannie says. I squirt a thin red line down her bun, sidestep a swarm of bees, and stuff my back pocket with paper napkins before returning to her, pleased with myself for finally catching on. "Here." Frannie takes the hot dog and I retreat behind the stroller, ready to head out. Two steps later a howl reaches my ears.

"What now?" I lean down toward Frannie.

"Bumblebee." And there is her hot dog on the grass with two bees crawling around the bun.

"Let's just go to the park," I say. "I'll buy you something to eat on the way." I reach into my back pocket for a napkin, marveling at the fact that even though Frannie was unable to take a bite out of her hot dog, she did manage to get a glob of ketchup in her ear. I wipe her face and steer her back to the car, stealing a glance at my watch. How can it possibly be only two-thirty-five? I can't take her back to Maria's yet. We haven't even been gone an hour.

I open the car door and a gust of heat hits me in the face like hot air from a blow dryer. I buckle Frannie into her car seat, untie her balloon, retie it to the handle of the back door, open the window of the driver's seat, collapse the stroller, stash it in the trunk, pop Frannie's bottle into her mouth, slide behind the wheel, start the car and head for the park.

"Window up," Frannie says from her perch in the back.

"You want the window up, Frannie?" I roll it up, then crack it, as the air in the car is really stifling.

"Window up. Window up." Frannie's high pitched voice is reaching new heights.

"Honey, I have to have the window cracked. It's ninety-eight degrees in here."

"Up. Up!" Frannie is screaming.

"Are you afraid your balloon will fly away again? I tied it." Frannie is screaming too loudly to hear me, but nevertheless, I continue. "Are you afraid a bumblebee will get into the car?" Frannie yells even louder. I roll the window down a little more to let the sound out. "I'm sorry, sweetie, you can't always have things your way." Now I sound exactly like my own mother. Oh well. She always did say when I had a child I would understand.

I drive by the school yard, also know as the park, only to find half the grass dug up and a noisy yellow tractor moving along on its gigantic wheels. I am a little disappointed and a lot relieved. "Looks like the park's closed today, Frannie. We'll have to go home."

"Swings. I want swings." Frannie points out the window.

"Sorry, toots. Not today. We'll have to go on the swings another time."

"Swings. Swings." She continues to cry as I steer the car back to Maria and Stephanie's, one hand on the wheel, one hand stroking her leg. Finally, one block from home, when I think my head is just about to implode, Frannie falls asleep.

I pull into the driveway and open the car door as quietly as possible. Frannie is dead weight in my arms as I lift her out of her car seat. I nudge the door with my hip just at the moment that Frannie's balloon decides to peek its stupid little red head out of the car. Of course the door shuts right on it. I hold my breath as the noise startles Frannie's eyes open. All is quiet for one lovely second and then all hell breaks loose.

"Go ahead and cry, Frannie," I say, hoisting her onto my hip. My own eyes fill as well, for it is not only Frannie's balloon that has burst, but my own bubble as well. Being a mother isn't all it's cracked up to be, I realize, but much, much, much, much more, and I'd only tried it for an hour. I ring the bell to Maria and Stephanie's apartment. No answer. Stephanie is still at work, I know, and Maria is probably out enjoying the precious freedom I take for granted.

I walk with Frannie over to a little patch of grass beside the driveway and sit down to wait for someone to come home. I am absolutely exhausted. I guess my decision not to have a child is the right one after all, I think, looking down at Frannie who has just fallen back asleep with her head on my shoulder and her arms around my neck. I stroke her back and she sighs contentedly, clinging to me as my heart turns over, heavy with the dearness of her and the weight of my choice.

Women's Rites

"C'mon, Jocelyn. Get wet." Andrea clasps her hands at the surface of the pool and squeezes her palms together, causing a spray of water to smack her best friend's thigh.

"Cut it out, Andrea. You're worse than the boys." Jocelyn, who is perched at the ledge of the shallow end, slaps at the water with a painted toenail. "I don't want to get my hair wet," she says, tossing the coif it has taken her all morning to comb, brush, wash, dry, set and spray.

"Okay, okay." Andrea throws her braid over her shoulder and dog paddles to the deep end where Tommy Battista and his buddies are romping in the chlorine like puppies. She joins them for a rousing game of monkey-in-the-middle, while Jocelyn slides the straps of her two piece down her sweaty shoulders to avoid a dreaded tan line. She leans back on her elbows, lifting her face to the sun, and as if that's some kind of signal, all the boys swim toward Jocelyn, splashing and yelling, pulling on her legs and finally dragging her into the water. Jocelyn screams like she's supposed to; half annoyed and half pleased. "You guys! My hair!" She scrambles out of the pool and grabs a towel. Andrea gets out too, shaking her wet braid at Jocelyn. She laughs at Jocelyn's little shriek, but no one else does. All the boys are staring up at Andrea from the ledge of the pool, which is odd, as they are usually much more interested in Jocelyn.

What gives, Andrea wants to ask, but something in their faces stops her. Finally Tommy Battista speaks. "Kind of nippy out today, huh Andrea?" he asks with a grin.

"What?" Andrea is puzzled. It's at least ninety degrees. She looks at Jocelyn, whose face is all crumpled together in an expression of sheer horror.

"Andrea." Jocelyn puts her arm across her friend's shoulders and turns around so both their backs are toward the boys. "You can see right through your bathing suit," she whispers. "*Everything*. You're supposed to put band-aids over them." She points to her own flat chest. "See?" But Andrea doesn't see a thing. She grabs her towel and races home, leaving her flip-flops behind, not even noticing the hot tar of the road is burning her feet. She dashes up the steps into the bathroom, and shuts the door to study herself in the full length mirror behind it.

It's absolutely true. There, under her brand new, canary-yellow, wet one piece for all the world to see, are her two erect-from-the-cold-water nipples, prominent as two Hershey's kisses atop a golden sponge cake. Andrea stares at her reflection. The two eyes of her nipples stare back. What is she going to do? Andrea wants to die, but she doesn't die. Instead she goes downstairs to show her mother, who decides they will go bra shopping that very afternoon.

"But Ma, I don't need a bra," Andrea tries to protest. "I just need a different bathing suit."

"We'll get you a new suit," Mrs. Greene replies. "But it's time for you to start dressing like a young lady."

"Ma-a," Andrea whines. "Me and the guys were gonna play running bases this afternoon."

"And acting like a young lady," Mrs. Greene continues. "Like your friend, Jocelyn. How come I haven't seen her around for a while ? You two have a fight?"

"No." Andrea shakes her head. "Ma, Jocelyn is getting so boring lately. All she ever wants to do is paint her nails and set her hair." Andrea rolls her eyes.

"What's so terrible about that?" Mrs. Greene asks. "Come on, I'll take you out for a sundae after."

"Okay." Andrea gives in, for after today's poolside adventure, she's not terribly anxious to meet up with the boys so soon again anyway.

They drive to the mall, park and head for Macy's, with Andrea lagging behind, pretending great interest in the back-to-school displays, the shoe stores, the record shop, anything to keep a respectable distance between her and her mother, so no one would know she was actually out on a Saturday afternoon with one of her parental units.

Mrs. Greene waits for her daughter at the entrance to Macy's. "We'll start with a training bra," she says.

Training for what, Andrea wants to know, but she doesn't ask. They find the lingerie department and Andrea's mother starts sorting through bins of pastel colored brassieres.

"What's lingerie?" Andrea asks, pronouncing the word with a hard G.

"Lin-ger-ie." Mrs. Greene corrects her. "It means women's underwear."

"Then why don't they just call it the underwear department?" Andrea asks.

"Because," her mother fishes out a pink bra trimmed with lace, "boys wear underwear. Girls wear panties."

"Then why don't they call it the panties department?"

Mrs. Greene pauses, up to her elbows in yellow, white, pink, peach and pale blue polyester. "Andrea, please."

A saleswoman approaches them with a tape measure draped around her neck like a snake. "Can I be of some assistance?" she asks.

"My daughter is here to buy her first bra," Mrs. Greene says. Andrea winces with embarrassment, but her mother sounds pleased, proud even, as if Andrea has done something remarkable.

"Isn't that wonderful?" the saleswoman says, and before Andrea can ask her what's so wonderful about it, she whips the tape measure off her neck and around Andrea's back and across her chest like a lasso. Andrea is very conscious of the slight pressure of the plastic strip against her nipples. "Thirty-two." The saleswoman beams at Andrea's mother as though they are old friends. "Those are over here." She hands Mrs. Greene several bras and leads them to the dressing room.

"I'll come in with you," Mrs. Greene says to her daughter.

"Ma, please." Andrea takes the bras and steps inside a mirrored cubicle, pulling a heavy beige curtain between her mother and herself. Andrea takes off her T-shirt, puts her arms through the straps of the bra, hoists it onto her shoulders and pulls the cups down over her barely budding breasts. Now for the tricky part: hooking the back. Andrea reaches behind herself and tries for several minutes, her arms flapping up and down like two useless wings.

"How is it?" her mother asks from behind the curtain. "Do you need some help?"

"Just wait a minute," Andrea snaps. She takes the bra off and studies it. Then some ancient, genetic female wisdom springs forth from her body to teach her what women have known forever: how to hook the bra at her waist, swivel it around to the back, put her arms through the straps and pull it onto her shoulders.

"Can I come in?" Without waiting for an answer, Mrs. Greene sweeps open the curtain with one arm, like a stage hand in an old musical. She stops and studies her daughter in the three-way, full length mirror. "Let me see," she says, pulling on Andrea's arms which are crossed in front of her chest.

Slowly Andrea unfolds her arms and drops them to her sides. She stares at her own reflection and at her mother's face floating in the mirror above it. Mrs. Greene looks stunned, then pleased, and then for a quick instant, terribly sad. For a minute Andrea is afraid she's done something wrong, but before she can ask what, Mrs. Greene turns from the mirror and busies herself with the bra, first loosening the straps, then tightening them again. "There," she says, stepping back as though she has just created a masterpiece. "How does that feel?"

"Fine," Andrea lies, for the truth is the elastic band underneath the cups is cutting into her rib cage and the side seams are digging a trench into her flesh.

"Do you want to try the other ones on?" Mrs. Greene asks.

""No, let's just take this." Andrea gets dressed while her mother pays for the bra and two others just like it. They leave the store and walk back through the mall side by side.

"Let's go to Friendly's," Mrs. Greene says, gesturing with the Macy's bag.

"No thanks," Andrea mumbles.

"Are you sure?" Mrs. Greene slows down in front of the ice cream shop. "It's a special day. Don't you want to celebrate?"

Andrea frowns at her mother. "C'mon Ma, let's just go home. I'm not in the mood."

"All right." Mrs. Greene drives home and Andrea takes the Macy's bag upstairs to her room where she cuts the price tags off all the brassieres. Then she puts on one of the bras and slides her favorite light blue tank top over it. It doesn't look any different except her bra strap shows. Andrea moves the strap over to the corner where her arm and shoulder meet, but it soon slides down the smooth flesh of her upper arm. There must be a trick to this, Andrea thinks, and then she remembers seeing Jocelyn pinning her bra straps to the strap of her sundress in the locker room after gym. Andrea goes into her mother's closet where she keeps her sewing box. Two safety pins do the trick all right, but now the silver metal of the pins show. She takes the elastic off the bottom of her braid and combs her hair out over her shoulders with her fingers. There. Now everything is covered.

Andrea stares at herself in the mirror, turning this way and that. She arches her back, places her hands on her hips and puckers up her mouth into a kiss, just as she has seen Jocelyn do. Andrea doesn't recognize the person in the mirror. She doesn't look like someone Andrea would ever want to meet, let alone be. But at the same time, it is hard to turn away from her.

"Andrea, supper," Mrs. Greene calls from downstairs. Andrea snaps out of her daze and changes back into her T-shirt. She opens the top drawer of her dresser where she keeps her underwear and undershirts and puts her new bras away. What should I do with my undershirts now, Andrea wonders. She takes them out of the drawer and sits on the edge of her bed, refolding them one by one. They are clean, fresh-smelling and soft. Andrea lifts the pile onto her lap and strokes the white fabric like some sort of beloved family pet. Her hand moves back and forth over the cool cotton, lulling her, almost hypnotizing her. Then she begins to cry very, very quietly, without knowing why.

Less Ugly

Chocolate pudding had just been passed out and the Minnows at the next table were busy flinging it at each other when Sam stood up and Marlene stopped breathing. Marlene was in love with Sam, with his stringy blonde hair and wire-rimmed glasses, with his long slender fingers and the way he'd wrap them around the neck of his Martin guitar, with his twangy voice which Marlene insisted was fifty times better than Bob Dylan's any day. But Sam didn't know Marlene was alive, he being a senior counselor and all, and she, like me being a lowly Trout, which wasn't as bad as being a Minnow, but still it would be two years until we were Dolphins and some of the Dolphins went out with counselors on the sly even though they weren't supposed to, especially since three years ago a girl got pregnant under a canoe and her parents sued Camp Wildwood for almost a million dollars. At least that's what Tina Jacobs said and she was a wealth of such vital information. She's the one who informed me that anything over a mouthful's a waste anyway the first time she saw me in a bathing suit, but Marlene said she was just jealous because Tina was as flat as the postcards our counselors handed out every Friday so we could write to our parents and tell them what a great time we were having or something to that effect if we wanted to help ourselves to a make-your-own-sundae at nine o'clock in the canteen.

Anyway, like I said, Sam stood up, cleared his throat and held up a plastic baggy full of cigarette butts. The usual roar of the dining room fell to a hushed din as Sam dramatically turned the baggy upside-down and dumped its contents onto the wooden floor. "I don't

smoke," he said, and for one second the room was silent except for
Marlene's sigh of utter ecstasy. Then Sam sat down and the general
chaos of two-hundred campers and counselors started up again

"Oh Marlene." I lowered my glasses to the tip of my nose and
looked over their tortoise shell rims at her in mock dismay. She was
still staring at Sam, her eyes huge and liquidy, like two pools of chocolate pudding about to ooze down her face. Sam was now biting into
an organic Macintosh apple he had fished out of his Save-A-Tree can-
vas backpack and Marlene pushed her pudding away. "What?" she
asked, turning to me. "I can dream, can't I?"

"Sure," I said, sliding my glasses back up my nose, the better-to-
see-you-with,-my-dear. I was doing plenty of dreaming myself that
summer, but not about Sam or Larry or Wayne or Roger or even
Claude, the swimming counselor who had given his whistle to Tina
Jacobs to wear around her neck. No, I had it bad, and I mean B-A-D
for Barney.

Barney. First of all she had straight brown hair all the way down
to the bottom of her shorts. Sometimes she wore it loose and sometimes she wore it in one braid down her back, swinging like the rope
to the dinner bell we all took turns pulling on to see who could make
it ring the loudest. Second of all, she had light blue eyes, the color of
a husky dog's. And third of all, her skin was the color of a marshmal-
low toasted to perfection over a Saturday night campfire when I was
lucky enough to be sitting on a log right next to her, so who cared if
some stupid Flying Fish got half his some'more stuck in my hair?
Barney was absolute perfection in her white shorts that frayed at the
bottom just right, and her blue T-shirt that matched her eyes, and her
cotton socks, one hugging the tight muscles of her calf, the other
rolled down twice to meet the rim of her black high-top sneaker. God,
I wanted to be just like her. But how could I be? Try as I might, my
hair would frizz up thirty seconds after I unrolled it from the coffee
can I set it around every night. Not to mention the fact that unless I
drenched myself in Coppertone my skin turned an early shade of
ketchup after two minutes in the sun. And then of course there were
my ugly, ugly, ugly, ugly glasses which hopefully would be replaced by

contact lenses next summer, if not before.

Anyway, Barney didn't seem to worry about what she looked like. I mean, after all she was perfect, so there was nothing much to worry about anyway, but still, she didn't spend too much time hanging out with the other girl counselors who were always painting their nails and pouring peroxide into their hair to streak it. Barney didn't have time for that stuff. She was too busy tossing around a Frisbee or oiling her mitt or fixing the volley ball net. That's another reason I liked her so much. She was like one of the guys. So much so, they let her play in the annual Wildwood versus White Birch Counselor Softball Game, which was *the* event of the summer.

The Saturday of the game, me and Marlene walked down to the softball field right after lunch to get a good seat. We plopped down on the grass right behind and a little to the left of home plate, as far from Tina Jacobs and her crowd as possible. Our team was warming up; Barney had all her hair tucked inside a New York Yankees baseball cap and Sam had a black elastic band attached to the ear pieces of his glasses, anchoring them to his head. Soon two yellow school buses full of White Birch campers and counselors arrived. After the campers got settled and the counselors warmed up, it was time to start the game.

Barney of course was spectacular. She played first base and every time the ball came her way she'd just lift her hand up in the air as easy as you please, just like she was waving hello to me, and the ball would smack into her glove and the ump would yell, "OUT!" jerking his thumb over his shoulder. Once Barney caught a ball to first and quick as a flash threw it to Sam who tagged the runner out at second and Marlene and I jumped up hugging each other tight and screaming so loud we practically busted each other's ear drums.

Then all of a sudden it was the bottom of the last inning. The score was tied eleven-eleven, bases loaded, two outs and Barney's turn to bat. Oh please God, please God, don't let her strike out, I prayed, closing my eyes for the briefest of seconds. Barney dusted off home plate, shifted her hips from side to side, and swung her bat up to her shoulder. The pitcher let the ball fly. Barney watched it, but didn't move.

"Strike one."

Oh Barney, Barney, Barney, don't fail me now. Sam was standing behind the third base line, giving Barney encouragement. "That's it, Barney. Don't swing on anything. You pick it now. You're a hitter. You're a hitter." The Wildwoodians were screaming, "We want a pitcher, not a glass of water," as the ball beelined to Barney, who again did not move.

"Strike two." I clutched Marlene's arms with both hands, almost cutting off the circulation between her elbow and her wrist. What was Barney doing? She had to swing at this one. The pitcher pitched, the ball zoomed at Barney, she swung and smack! that ball was gone— over the pitcher's head, over second base, and way past the outfielder, who leaped up in the air with his glove extended anyway, before turning around and making a dash for it.

Meanwhile, Barney tossed her bat aside and loped around the bases graceful as the deer we had seen last week on an overnight in the backwoods. The outfielder finally caught up with the ball and threw it to second. By this time, everyone had come home except for Barney, who was rounding third. The second baseman threw the ball wildly at the catcher. It made a wide arc in the sky, then hung suspended in the air for a second, completely blocking the sun like an eclipse before hurling itself downward, straight for me.

"Heads up, heads up," someone yelled at the same time I said to Marlene, "That ball's gonna hit me in the face." And sure enough, one second later that softball which was anything but soft, caught me right between the eyes and cracked my glasses right in two, clean as a twig someone snapped in half before tossing it into the campfire. And so I was glasses-free and just a tiny bit less ugly for the rest of that summer, so who cared that the only thing I could see clearly from then on until I went home was Barney's face, two inches from mine, her hair spilling out of her cap and brushing against my cheek, her blue eyes filled with delicious concern as she asked me over and over, "Are you all right? Are you all right?"

Mom, Dad and Ralph

My father stood in the door frame between the living room and the kitchen in his London Fog raincoat and gray felt hat, his briefcase still in his hand.

"Does Ralph have to go O-U-T?"

My mother lifted her eyes from the six o'clock news and impaled them upon my father's face. "I took him about an hour ago."

"Did he make?"

If my mother answered no, that was the end of the discussion. If she answered yes, further questioning ensued: "Did he make a lot? Did he make good? Does he have to make again?" In either case, the conversation would end with my father asking, "Ralphie, wanna go out?" and at the utterance of the word *out*, Ralph would fly off my mother's lap and dance in circles on the blue shag rug until my father managed to hook his leash onto Ralph's collar and lead him out the front door.

When they returned, after ten minutes or so, it was my mother who began the line of questioning.

"So, *nu*, did he make?"

If my father answered, "He *pished* a little, but he didn't make," my mother would say, "All right, maybe he'll make later." But if my father entered the house announcing, "He made!" great fanfare ensued. Ralph would gallop into the living room and leap onto my mother's lap as if he hadn't seen her in days. My mother would gaze into Ralph's eyes crooning, "What a good boy. Yes, yes, you are. What a good boy. Such a good boy." My father would join them in the living room, still in his hat and coat, also singing Ralph's praises. Then my mother would say, "Give him some crackers. He's such a good boy." And my father would be off to the kitchen with Ralph at his heels, to dispense three liver-flavored crackers, shaped like a fireman, a policeman and a mailman.

"Did he eat?" my father would call, for Ralph's dish was always empty, either because he hadn't been fed yet (a rare occasion) or more likely, because he had been fed and his bowl had been licked clean thirty seconds after the food had hit the dish.

"I fed him at four o'clock," my mother's voice drifted in over the sportscaster's, "but if he ate it all, you could give him a little *nosh.*"

And so my father would dollop a plop of Alpo into Ralph's dish, which he ate gleefully, his tail to the wind. Of course this meant that Ralph would have to go O-U-T again in about an hour, after my father had taken off his hat and coat, eaten dinner, read the newspaper, and perhaps moved his own bowels as well.

And so I learned the importance of consistency as the cycle of ingesting and eliminating continued, with interruptions occurring only rarely, due to an occasional breakdown in Ralph's plumbing system. I don't recall Ralph ever being constipated, though if he were, a tablespoon of prune juice, an eyedropper of Pepto Bismal, or an enema administered by my mother would certainly have cured him. Once in a great while, however, Ralph did suffer from bouts of diarrhea. During these times my mother would cook up a small pot of rice, which was said to be binding, and mix it with a little chopped sirloin. Cheese, bananas and *matzo* were also rumored to be binding, but I can't recall Ralph ever being offered those particular items.

When Ralph suffered from indigestion, my father's after work interrogation became even more intense. "Did he make today? How was it? What time? What color? Hard or soft? Did he strain? He only made once today? Are you sure? Maybe he has to make again. Ralphie, wanna go out?"

And so it went on for fourteen years, until one day Ralph made on the rug, something he hadn't done since the days of young puppydom. My mother got down on her hands and knees (something she hadn't done since puppy days either), cleaned the rug, and comforted Ralph. "Poor old puppy, you don't feel so good today, do you Ralph? That's okay. You just rest."

When my father came home and asked, "Does Ralph have to go O-U-T?" my mother replied, "No, he made already. On the rug."

"He made on the rug?" My father looked at Ralph and then at my mother. "What's the matter, is he sick? Did he eat today? Did he drink water? Where on the rug?"

My mother pointed to a dark spot on the blue shag and my father took two steps toward it and then stopped. "Do you think I should take him O-U-T?" he asked.

"Ralphie," my mother addressed the puddle of fur on her lap. "Do you want to go out?"

Ralph's ears twitched but the rest of him remained still.

"Maybe later," my mother said. "Let him rest for now."

For the next two months, Ralph made in the house almost every day. My mother put a thick layer of newspaper down over one corner of the rug and changed it whenever necessary. My father still asked if Ralph had to go out (spelling now become unnecessary, for Ralph's incontinence had been accompanied by an acute loss of hearing) and if he had made that day. A new question joined the repertoire. If my mother answered, "Yes, he made," my father would ask "Where?" "On his newspaper," my mother answered, to which my father always responded, "What a good boy."

And then one day in the middle of an afternoon nap on the couch, Ralph heaved a great sigh, whimpered once, and died. My mother called the vet who sent someone to fetch him and then she called my father at the office. When my father came home that evening, he stood in the door frame between the kitchen and the living room as usual, his hat on his head, his London Fog belted at the waist, his briefcase in hand. My mother didn't look at him but he could see her eyes were red. Her hands were in her lap, her left on top of her right, her fingers making minute circles on her flesh as if she were stroking the small space between Ralph's ears.

"He was a good boy, wasn't he?" my father asked softly.

"He was a very good boy," my mother answered quietly.

"He never made in the house until the end," my father said, "and that wasn't his fault."

"No, that wasn't his fault," my mother said. "He couldn't help it."

"No," my father agreed, "he couldn't help it. He was always a good boy."

"Yes," said my mother, "a very good boy."

Eventually my father put down his briefcase and removed his hat and coat. Eventually my mother served supper. Life continued. Eventually Ralph's dish was taken off the kitchen floor, washed, dried and put away. His leash was retired to the top shelf of the hall closet. Life went on. Eventually I left home and learned to make do on my own. I don't think my father and mother noticed. I hear from them once a year; on my birthday they send a small check enclosed in a Snoopy card. The check is always signed by my father, and the card by my mother: With best wishes, Mom, Dad and Ralph.

PART II: HALFWAY TO HEAVEN

My Tropical Butch

for Mary Grace Vazquez

My tropical butch has spit shiny black hair with eyes to match and dark skin the color of honey which is what she lets me call her when no one else is around. My tropical butch is all woman even though she spills her change out of her front pocket onto the dresser when she gets home from work just like my daddy did and combs her short black hair back from her forehead just so with one hand chasing the other all the way around to the back of her perfectly shaped head. And even though some stupid man says, "Yes sir?" when we pull up to his gas pump in her shiny red car, my tropical butch is all woman and don't you forget it, especially on a Saturday night in July like tonight when it's ninety-five degrees in the shade even though the sun went down hours ago when we were sitting on the front porch eating rice and beans and drinking piña coladas out of each other's eyes.

On a night like tonight, even though the air is thick as coconut milk, my tropical butch puts on her white pants, black shirt, white jacket and Panama hat and I know she wants me in a little red dress with shoes to match and earrings that bounce off my shoulders and hair that trickles all the way down my back because it's Saturday night and my tropical butch is taking me out to a little place in the city she knows where we can salsa, mambo and meringue all night long, since my tropical butch thinks dancing way across the room from each other with our hands and feet flapping is a major waste of time.

When a slow grinding song comes on, my tropical butch holds me real tight and shrugs her shoulders so my whole arm slips up around

45

her neck, first the right one, then the left, and then she puts a little kiss on my collarbone and slides her leg between my thighs and if I don't cut myself on the razor sharp crease of her bright, white pants, I tell you I am halfway to heaven.

Then we leave the bar and kiss in the parking lot and my tropical butch tastes salty and sweet as the Caribbean, and there's a little breeze now blowing my hair back like leaves on a palm tree and soon we're both wet as a rain forest so we get back in her little red car and speed down the highway with my head on my tropical butch's shoulder and her hand on my thigh and then some.

When we get home we leave a trail of clothes all through the house: my high heels at the front door, my little red dress in the kitchen, my slip in the hall until we get to the bedroom and all I got on is my earrings. My tropical butch still looks as fresh as when we left the house of course, except for the red lipstick I left all over her face in the moonlight.

Now comes the best part. My tropical butch lays me down and takes her own sweet time exploring every inch of me like I'm her very own island that she's been away from for far too long and ain't it good to be back home. And after she moves over me fierce as a hurricane and gentle as an island breeze, my tropical butch lets me undress her so I can remember that she is all woman even though she bought the pants I just unzipped in the men's department at JC Penney's and even though the shirt I just unbuttoned would never be mistaken for a blouse, my tropical butch is all woman with a body that just won't quit until all the stars in the night sky have disappeared and the sun's just starting to come up over the horizon glowing a deep reddish-orange like a rich, ripe papaya to find me and my tropical butch sleeping all curled together like two gorgeous parrots high in the top of some palm tree where no one will ever, ever find us.

How To Make Your Lover Miss You

When your lover tells you she has to fly off to Berkeley or Chicago or Somewheresville, PA, don't look disappointed or tell her not to go. Offer to pack her suitcase instead. Iron her slacks so neatly they lay on top of each other flat as love letters waiting for her to lift out one by one by one. Under her slacks, place the red silk teddy you bought her for Valentine's Day and the black lace slip you gave her for your last anniversary. Slip a photo of you in her toiletry bag, the one where you're wearing that hat you think looks awfully silly but she thinks looks awfully sexy. Dab a bit of your perfume on her pajamas so she'll dream about you all night long.

When you're done packing, make wild passionate love to her, even though you're exhausted and she's got other things on her mind. Hold her in your arms all night long, even though it might mean an emergency visit to the chiropractor to work out that kink in your spine. Drive her to the airport in the morning, keeping one hand on the steering wheel and the other on her thigh. Hug her tightly, but don't say, "Call me when you get there so I know you're safe." Instead say, "Call me after eleven when the rates go down." Don't smooth away the furrow that instantly appears between her eyebrows with your loving fingertips.

When the phone rings at 11:01, let the answering machine pick it up. Sit on your hands when she moans, "Where *are* you?" and wait a good fifteen minutes before you call her back. Don't tell her you were taking a bath. Say you were lonely so you went to the movies by yourself, and wouldn't you know it, your ex was there, so after the film you went out for a drink and got to talking.... When your lover remains silent on the other end of the phone, wait a good seven seconds before you change the subject and ask how her trip is going. When she starts giving you details about the presentation she gave to the entire board of directors, interrupt her to remind her how expensive long distance phone calls are. Don't say "I miss you" until she says it first.

When it's time to pick your lover up at the airport, meet her at the gate with one long-stemmed red rose. Give her a nice juicy kiss at the baggage claim, even though she hates public displays of affection. Carry her suitcase out to the car and drive down the freeway with one hand on the steering wheel and the other on her knee. When you get home, undress her and put her in the shower. Join her and wash the trip away. Don't forget to scrub her everywhere.

The next time your lover tells you she has to go on a business trip, don't look disappointed or tell her not to go. Offer to pack her suitcase instead. Don't act surprised when she calls from work and tells you she's not going. In a concerned voice, ask her why. Try not to gloat when she tells you she told her boss she has more important business to take care of at home.

Red, White and Absolutely Blue

You want to know why I'm eating blue spaghetti with tomato sauce and tofu all by myself on the fourth of July? There's a simple, logical, one word explanation: Margaret.

She left me. I was looking forward to spending a whole day with her smack dab in the middle of the week. You know, we'd get up late, make love, hang out, drink coffee, go back to bed, have a picnic, watch the fireworks. Well, that was the plan, but it seems my Margaret was off somewhere making fireworks of her own. With someone else. And like a poorly written soap opera, I was the last to know.

So, while the rest of Boston was celebrating the birth of our nation (or protesting it, whatever turns you on) I was alone. All by myself with no picnic ingredients, no party to go to, no one to ooh and aah with down at the Esplanade when it got dark and they shot those babies up into the air.

So, I moped around most of the day feeling sorry for myself, and then at about five o'clock I snapped out of it. I mean, I had no right to fall into the pity pot. I was young, healthy, employed and reasonably good looking, with a roof over my head and food on the table. That's when I decided, what the heck, I'd make myself a festive meal and have a private celebration. Hell, I'm a woman of the nineties. I don't need anyone else, right? I can take care of myself.

So, due to the day being what it was, and me being the cornball that I am, the meal had to be red, white and blue. I opened the refrigerator and immediately saw red: a jar of Paul Newman's tomato sauce. Perfect. Red was for blood, anger, revenge, how dare that bitch leave me for somebody else? I'm the best thing that ever happened to her. And she knew it, too. Or used to know it.

Now I was feeling blue. Blue food was trickier. I didn't have any blueberries in the fridge. On to the pantry. Would navy beans count? Hardly. How about a can of green beans? Almost, but not quite. Although some people have trouble telling the difference between blue and green and some people don't even think there is a difference. I found that out a few years ago when I was waiting for the T at Harvard Square. A music student from Japan struck up a conversation with me, pointing at my sweater with her flute case. "That's a nice green sweater," she said, though my sweater happened to be blue. When I told her that, she smiled and said there was only one word for blue and green in Japanese, which sounded quite lovely and meant the color of the water. I started wishing my subway would never come, but of course it did, and off I went, only to meet Margaret three days later as a matter of fact. But I refuse to think about that now. Anyway, the point is, if I was Japanese, the green beans would do just fine, but then again, if I was Japanese, I'm sure I wouldn't give a flying fuck about the fourth of July.

Back to the pantry. That's when I spotted those little bottles full of food coloring: red, green, yellow and blue. I'd gotten them last year for St. Patrick's Day, to make bona fide green mashed potatoes for Margaret. The blue bottle was still full. What could I dye with it?

Why, spaghetti, of course. We used to color spaghetti when I taught day care. We'd save this special activity for a freezing Friday in February when the kids were off the wall from being cooped up all week, and the teachers were going bananas from five days of dealing with seventeen pairs of mittens, boots, snow pants, scarves, sweaters, hats and jackets. To while away the afternoon, we'd cook up a huge vat of spaghetti, dye it different colors and throw it against the wall, where it would stick, making a mural I'm sure Picasso himself would have been proud of.

I put up a pot of water, contemplating blue: sadness, an ocean of tears, Lady Day singing the blues, red roses for a blue lady, that was me all right. Sigh.

Two down and one to go. White. Like every good dyke, I didn't have any white bread, white flour, white sugar or white rice in my cupboard, but I did have that handy dandy item that no lesbian household is complete without: a virgin block of tofu sitting on the top shelf of the refrigerator in a bowl of water. I chopped it up, thinking about white: a blank page, empty space, tabula rasa, clean sheets, starting over, yeah.

So I set the table and sat down with my very own red, white and blue meal, feeling angry, empty and sad. To tell you the truth, the plate in front of me wasn't very appealing. I took a bite anyway and swallowed. Not too bad, actually. A little chewy maybe, but other than that, okay. After I forced four bites down past the lump in my throat, it hit me: it wasn't just the fourth of July I was celebrating; it was Independence Day. I was celebrating my independence by eating a completely ridiculous meal and the best part about it was I didn't have to explain it or justify it or defend it or hide it or even share it with anyone. I tell you, the fifth bite was delicious, and after that the food just started tasting better and better. As a matter of fact, I don't remember spaghetti ever tasting so good. I had seconds and then thirds. I ate it with my fingers, I let the sauce drip down my chin, I picked up the plate and licked it clean. Yum, yum, yum. My country 'tis of me.

Comfort

You had been on your way to do an errand, though now you can't remember what it was you'd needed. A box of envelopes perhaps, or a roll of tape. But you'd turned the corner and there SHE was, the woman you'd had a crush on for over a year. She was staring into the window of a café trying to decide whether or not to go in maybe, but no, actually she was studying her own reflection you realized, for she reached up and tucked one stubborn piece of hair under her beret. You loved her for that. Then she opened the door to the café and went in and you sighed and walked on, knowing you probably wouldn't catch sight of her again for another three months, probably not until spring.

So you walked on and got your stamps or your menstrual pads or whatever it was, and on the way back you found yourself entering that very same café which was odd, because you are not a café sort of person. You much prefer a twenty-four hour diner with coffee and home-made apple pie to cappuccino and Black Forest cake. But there you were, with a cup of Mocha Java of all things in your hand, looking around for a place to sit. There were no empty tables and as you pondered your situation, SHE looked up at you and smiled. Was that an invitation? Later you'd say it was and she would deny it, but nevertheless, you found yourself floating toward the empty chair opposite her. Floating, I say, because your feet were not touching the ground.

"Do you mind if I sit down?" you asked.

She shook her head and the silver earrings she wore rang like little bells. She was reading a thick book you couldn't see the title of, but you thought she was probably an English major with her earrings and beret and all. She didn't return to her book, but put a feather in the page to mark her place and then slapped it shut as though she'd been waiting for you to arrive, and was even in fact a little annoyed that you were late.

"I'm Alexandria," she said, extending a delicate hand. You took it, wondering what to do with it, tempted to bring her hand up to your lips and kiss it, but you just held it gently.

"I'm Jackie," you said, amazed that you remembered your own name, amazed that it hadn't changed as you felt the rest of you had. Somehow you knew your whole life would be different from this moment on. Her hand was soft, her fingers slim, and she wore one silver ring with a blue stone in it. She took her hand back and smiled and you stared at her mouth as if you had never seen a mouth before, as if you'd never noticed now wonderful it was the way lips curve over teeth, the red against the white. Suddenly you realized you were staring so you looked down at your own hands, which seemed big and clumsy by comparison, and you didn't look up again until you felt your blush subside.

She asked you questions and you answered them: you told her about your life, you suppose, about growing up in a small town and always feeling different, about running away to a big city and your first awful year when you lived in that rooming house with no kitchen and the bathroom down the hall and the man next door who hung his bananas on a rope strung from one end of his room to the other so the roaches wouldn't get them. All the while you were talking, you were thinking, I sound so dumb, I'm talking too much, she must be bored by all this, but still you went on. You told her about hanging out in bars and how you didn't do that anymore and how you left the city and moved to this town five years ago with nothing in your pocket but the name and phone number of a high school friend who was rumored to be "different" as well.

So here you were, working as the maintenance person of your apartment building for free rent and working part-time at a print shop three days a week for spending money. Left you lots of time to think, you said. You were thinking of taking a computer course, you said, for you heard that's where the money was, the way of the future and all that.

She said she had a computer and did you want to see it? You blinked, not sure you heard right. Was she inviting you back to her room? Was this the modern day equivalent of *would you like to come up and see my etchings?* Maybe you were misinterpreting her, but you knew she was a lesbian by the labyris around her neck and you sure hoped she didn't smile at everyone the way she was smiling at you now. She stood, and you did too, though your knees were quite rubbery.

You followed her out the door and up the street, out of the downtown area, heading for the college. She talked about her computer some, how her father bought it for her, how easy it was to write papers now, and you realized she was probably nervous too. You wondered if she did this all the time, though you still weren't sure if she was thinking along the same lines as you. She was so pretty, even in that ridiculous hat and black sweater and purple boots. You thought she was nineteen, twenty at the most, but later she told you she was twenty-five, just a year younger than you. Her life hadn't been easy either, though she'd never had to worry about money the way you did. Her parents had found her in bed with her best friend her senior year of high school and the day after she graduated they kicked her out. Her father had been against it, but her mother stood firm. So her father kept in touch with her over the years, sending her money every month, trying to make up for her mother's disowning her. He was footing the bill for her tuition, even though this was her third try at college. And yes, she was an English major.

She led you to an old Victorian house. She had the attic apartment: two rooms and a bath. One room was the kitchen, and one room was everything else: living room, study and bedroom combined. In one corner was a stereo and a stack of records, across from that a desk with the now famous computer, and of course what your eyes were very busily avoiding: the bed. She closed the door behind you and kicked off her little purple boots, motioning for you to do the same. It felt like it took you hours to unlace your sneakers. Everything seemed to be moving in slow motion: the hands of the clock on the wall, Alexandria as she moved toward you and took your hand, the sun as it crept across the bed, first warming her belly, then her breasts, then her beautiful face as she lay next to you afterwards, half asleep, content as a cat that had just licked a bowl of cream.

You had never been more wide awake in your whole life. You had never done such a thing before: made love to a woman you hardly knew, a virtual stranger, in the middle of the afternoon. You had only had two other lovers; one in the city, an older woman who was married, and one who had broken your heart two years ago by leaving you for a close friend. You didn't think sex was all that important. You were a loner.

But she, well, you certainly never met anyone like her before. She was good at sex, the way one is good at cards, or playing the piano. You could tell it was something she did often. You didn't want her to do it with anyone but you. She laughed when you told her that. She put her arms around you and said she always wanted someone to love her enough to be jealous. You were surprised, for as she said the words you realized you did love her, even though you didn't believe in love at first sight. You believed you got to know a person slowly and you learned to love them day by day.

Which is exactly what happened. You saw each other every day and you slept together every night. Sometimes you made love and sometimes you didn't. Sometimes you just held her and stroked her hair away from her beautiful face and kissed her forehead. She said she felt safe with you. She said she trusted you because you had honest hands. Honest hands. You liked that.

You learned things about her. You learned she liked breakfast in bed on a wooden tray with a pink rose in a glass vase. You learned that she hated to cook and if left to her own devices would have popcorn for supper. You learned that she could wiggle her ears and raise one eyebrow at a time, that her favorite color was purple and that she didn't wear underwear in the summer under her long cotton dresses.

You taught her things, too. You taught her how to blink across the room at a cat and sit very still until it blinked back. You taught her how to seal up her windows for winter and how to plant morning glories along a fence for spring. You taught her how to find the constellations in the night sky, the Big Dipper, Cassiopeia's Throne, Orion's Belt, and how to wish upon a shooting star.

In the summer a tenant moved out of your building and she moved into it. A year after that you rented an apartment together. By now you were working full-time at the print shop and she had dropped out of school again. She got a job working in a day care center and you were afraid she'd want her own child, but she said no, you and the dog were quite enough, thank you, for you had gotten her a puppy for her birthday that year.

And so the days passed and the years passed and you were quite happy. You became a partner at the print shop and she opened her own child care center, after finally finishing her degree. You both worked hard, though you made sure you took plenty of vacations, too. One day you noticed some gray in her hair. One day she noticed your body had thickened, like the strong trunk of a tree. How had it happened? All of a sudden the puppy was an old dog with a white muzzle. And you were still happy.

You had managed to stay together all those years as you had watched other couples break up. Your friends split over monogamy and non-monogamy, wanting a child and not wanting a child, staying put or moving to California. And of course the big three: money, how much time to spend together, and sex. You didn't fight about money because you kept yours separate, and you didn't fight about how much time to spend together, because both of you wanted to spend all your time together. Sometimes you did quibble about sex, especially in the beginning, for she was much freer than you. But that had shifted and as a matter of fact, over the years you'd even managed to surprise her with a trick or two.

Sometimes lying in bed at night you'd wonder what your life would have been like if you hadn't wandered back to the café that day. What if she'd been sitting with someone else? What if she hadn't smiled? What if... But she would just shush you by putting her fingers against your lips. It was meant to be, she'd say, why question it? You weren't questioning the rightness of it, for you were sure about that. It was just that to you it was a miracle that all these years later she was still beside you at the breakfast table, she was still beside you in bed at night, she was still the very first thing you saw every blessed morning. And she, not that she took you for granted, but she accepted it more easily, as though she always knew this would happen to her, that one day the woman of her dreams would walk into her life and she would sweep her off her feet and they would live together happily ever after. And so you grew older and happier still, for every day with her added to your happiness. Even though you loved her with all your heart and all your soul and you couldn't imagine loving her any more than you already did, your love grew and grew.

And then all of a sudden it was time to retire, and there you were, two old ladies in flannel pajamas, laughing because you didn't know if these were your reading glasses or hers, and she couldn't remember whose teeth were in the pink glass on the bathroom sink. And then it wasn't funny anymore because you knew you would have to lose each other and you couldn't tell if it was better for you to die first, for how could you stand living without her; but then again perhaps she should go first, for you couldn't bear the thought of her being so sad without you.

You knew that you would always be together no matter what, so when the end came you were sad, terribly sad, but you did manage alone, just as you had done before her. You kept most of her things, including the beret she had worn that first day. Sometimes you held it on your lap and stroked it like a cat. Other days you spread the big picture album across your lap and there she was again, smiling into the camera, or shaking a finger at you, pretending to be cross, or arching her back with her hands on her hips in a Marilyn Monroe pose. Some days you did nothing but cry, and you would hear her voice out of nowhere scolding you gently, *now, now*, she would say, and you'd smile and then cry even harder.

Many of your friends were gone too, and those that weren't offered what comfort they could, but it wasn't much. You hadn't been big socializers, but instead had hoarded your precious free time to your-selves. Maybe you should have gone out with other people more, but no, you didn't regret one single second you had spent with her and if you had to do it all over again, you couldn't imagine changing a thing. And that was your comfort.

Monday Night At The Movies

I'm a girls-just-wanna-have-fun type of gal and so is my best friend, Nancy. When she left the Big Apple for the Pioneer Valley of western Massachusetts, the city just wasn't fun anymore.

"When are you coming back?" I yelled into the phone one Sunday morning, my left hand cupped over my free ear to drown out the siren wailing up Second Avenue.

"Never," Nancy said. "It's Paradise up here. I know you don't believe me, but really, there is life after the Rotten Apple."

No, I didn't believe her, but when I lost my job and got mugged in the same week, I figured I didn't have all that much to lose. So I joined Nancy in what they actually call the Happy Valley, and though the scenery is lovely and the lack of cockroaches divine, well, it's just kind of quiet around here, even for Paradise. I mean, there's just not that much to do for two good-time gals like us after ten o'clock at night. Or nine o'clock for that matter. For a while in December the stores downtown were open until nine-thirty and that was kind of exciting. But now it was January and all the holiday cheer was gone, leaving us with inflated VISA bills, single digit temperatures and not much else.

I was browsing through the Saturday paper one afternoon (there is no Sunday paper, if you can believe it) when an ad caught my eye: Movie Extras Wanted. Actors, Actresses, Musicians. No Experience Necessary. I called Nancy immediately. Of course she had clipped the ad, too.

"I can't wait to audition!" I yelled into the phone. "Maybe we'll meet Cher. Or Madonna!"

"I doubt it," Nancy said. "Don't you think they have better things to do than watch a bunch of wanna-be's make fools of themselves at the Springfield Ramada Inn on a Monday night?"

"Maybe they're looking for ethnic faces," I said hopefully: I'm Jewish and Nancy's Italian. We talked on the phone a few minutes longer and decided I would cook us dinner and Nancy would drive. We also decided our chances would improve if we each went as a type, and Nancy generously agreed to go frumpy so I could go glamorous. However, when Monday night rolled around and the temperature dropped below my shoe size, I decided to forego my sequined mini-dress in favor of an oversized sweater on top of tight, black leggings. Nancy showed up in an identical outfit and I pretended not to notice that my idea of glamour was the same as her idea of frump.

The ride took about half an hour and as we approached Springfield, our nervousness kicked in. "Do you think we have a chance?" I asked Nancy. "I mean, when I was a kid, this friend of my father's was always saying to me 'You oughtta be in pictures,' but he was just a creep who was always trying to pull me on his lap so he could play with my hair."

"The whole thing might be a scam," Nancy warned me as we pulled off the highway. "One of my co-workers went to one of these once and it turned out to be a recruitment session for a religious cult."

"Oh, great," I groaned, feeling like a fool already. "We'll probably be the only ones there."

Nancy pulled into a parking space and cut the engine. We each fussed with our hair and then stepped out into the wind which total-ly disheveled us. We ran for the hotel lobby, where a sign that simply said, "Casting" pointed us to the right.

After a quick trip to the women's room to check our lipstick, we rounded the corner and entered a ballroom filled with over two-hun-dred people of all shapes and sizes. Most of them were dressed to kill, and each of them was filling out a form. I asked a woman who looked like she'd used a magic marker to apply her eyeliner where she got her application. "Up there," she pointed with a number two pencil, "from the lady with the hair."

Nancy and I made our way up to the front of the room where the woman with "the hair" who did not look unlike Dolly Parton gave us an application and told us to get on line for an interview. We moved to the end of the room and I leaned on Nancy's back to fill out the form. Under "name" I put *Dolly Grip* as Nancy had made me promise not to sign anything. I filled out my address and phone number and pondered the only other question on the application: "Why do you think you can succeed in this business?" "Because I always succeed in everything I do," I wrote, thinking that after all, a movie star should exude confidence. Meanwhile, Nancy filled out her form in bright red lipstick, hoping that would make an impression.

We inched our way to the front of the room. I listened to the interview of the man in front of me, whose cologne was making me dizzy. "Ever acted before?" he was asked.

"Oh, yes," he said. "Shakespeare, Ibsen, Ionesco..."

"Fine, come back tomorrow for a screen test. Next," the interviewer barked, placing his paper to the left.

I pushed Nancy in front of me. The interviewer took her application without looking at it.

"Ever acted before?"

"No."

"Do any public speaking?"

"Oh yes, at my job I..."

"Great, have a seat. Next." He slid Nancy's paper to the right and took my application.

"Ever acted before?"

"No."

"Any musical talent?"

"No."

He made eye contact with me and as far as I could tell was not dazzled by my stunning good looks, as I had hoped. "Are you down here on a lark?"

"Yes," I stammered.

"Have a seat. Next." And he slapped my application down on top of Nancy's.

I sat down next to Nancy and we compared notes. "Why didn't he ask me about public speaking?" I moaned, crossing my legs at the ankles in case anyone was looking. Then I jumped up and made Nancy switch seats with me, since I look better from the right. She rolled her eyes, but humored me. We immediately struck up a conversation with the woman beside Nancy, who it turned out had once been on a local TV commercial. She immediately became the celebrity of our row: a man in front of her turned around to ask her what one should wear to a screen test and the woman behind Nancy leaned forward to listen to her reply. She said basic black was best but a man two seats down said stripes were definitely the way to go if you want to get attention. "Whatever you do, don't wear orange," a woman behind me said. Everyone had an opinion: I hadn't felt this much camaraderie since the last time I was in Manhattan riding a crosstown bus. The man to my left told me he was out of work and could use even a mere twenty bucks a day. "Good luck," I said. "You, too," he answered as we shook hands.

Then a hush came over the room as the man who had interviewed us rose wearily from his seat, grabbed a microphone and launched into his shpeel. He told us that going through a casting agency was the only way to break into the business and then proceeded to explain why this casting agency was the best. He told us that out of all the people sitting in the room, only about four or five had what it took to make it. He explained how hard the work was, and how much money we would need to spend traveling from set to set and printing up copies of our resumes and 8x10 glossies. I slouched down in my seat as he droned on, thinking, I missed *Murphy Brown* for this? Finally he rattled off the list of movies they would soon be casting for, in hopes no doubt of impressing us.

"But," our host said with a smile, "you know why you're all here, don't you? You're all being considered for *Nazi Lesbians From Hell.*"

As the room exploded in laughter, Nancy and I locked eyes: we are both lesbians. Suddenly we were no longer just one of the crowd, out on a lark or perhaps to pursue a dream. Suddenly we were *other*, feared and hated, the butt of everybody's joke. As people around us continued to chuckle, I felt sweat collecting under my sweater. The man to my left, who'd shaken my hand earlier, smiled at me. I didn't smile back. Would be have been so friendly if he knew? I wondered. Obviously he had no idea he was laughing at Nancy and me. We are both Glamour Dykes and would no sooner leave the house without lipstick than most people would leave the house without underwear. Consequently, we "pass." I can't speak for Nancy, but I know that ninety-nine percent of the straight people I meet assume I am one of their own, unless I inform them otherwise.

Our presenter continued his prepared speech, but I was no longer listening. Where is ACT-UP or Queer Nation when you need them, I wondered. I looked around the room. If the current statistics were true, then twenty of the two-hundred people sitting in that room were gay. Not to mention the fact that undoubtedly more than a few of us had gay friends, siblings, parents, uncles, aunts, neighbors, teachers, doctors, hairdressers, electricians, etc. etc. Were Nancy and I the only ones who found the presenter's joke unfunny? Had we truly turned into a pair of feminists with no sense of humor?

As our host's endless speech dragged on, I turned the phrase over in my mind. *Nazi Lesbians From Hell.* Nazi and Hell are synonymous with evil. *Am I so vile?* I wanted to scream. But I didn't scream. I said nothing.

After telling us for the last time how expensive this venture would be and how only two or three of us would make it, our host read off the chosen few who would appear tomorrow at two o'clock sharp for a screen test. He rattled off ninety-seven names.

"It's definitely a scam," Nancy whispered to me. "Why would they bother with so many people if only three of us have what it takes to make it?" I shrugged my shoulders; she continued thinking out loud. "They probably charge you for the screen test. Or make you buy one-hundred 8x10 glossies for ten bucks each. Or something."

We'll never know, as neither of our names were called. Nor was the man sitting next to me, whose smile had been replaced by a look of quiet desperation. The woman next to Nancy beamed and everyone wished her luck.

Nancy put on her coat and turned to me. "Ready?"

"One second," I said, and before I knew what I was doing, I made my way up to the front of the room.

"Excuse me." I stared at our casting director, who was now trying to fit his mike into its stand, like the movie star we all yearned to be.

"Yes?" He smiled and put his hand on my shoulder.

"I'm a Jew..." I said.

"Oy," he interrupted.

"...and," I swallowed hard, "I'm a lesbian, and..." I waited until he finished laughing. "And your joke really offended me."

His hand flew off my shoulder as his face snapped shut. "Listen, doll," he snarled, "this is my show and I'll say whatever the hell I want."

"I'm sure you will," I said. "I just needed to let you know." I walked away as he hurled some words at my back that I couldn't make out, which was probably just as well.

"What'd you say to him?" Nancy asked as we made our way back to the car. I repeated the conversation as we shivered in the front seat, waiting for the engine to warm up.

"Why didn't you tell me?" she asked. "I would have gone up with you."

"I don't know. I didn't think about it. I just did it."

"I am so proud of you." Nancy backed the car out of its parking space. "That was so brave."

I tried to shrug it off. "It's no big deal." I stared out the window, thinking. "It'll probably just add fuel to his fire. You know, the next time he says it, he'll probably add, 'and I did meet a Nazi Lesbian From Hell in Springfield, Massachusetts, and boy did she need a good...'"

"Never mind him," Nancy said, steering the car onto the road. "You didn't do it for him. You did it for yourself. For us. For every lesbian in that room. You did it so you could look yourself in the eye and not feel ashamed."

"Oh yeah?" I pulled the rearview mirror toward me as we waited at a red light and stared at my own reflection. What did I see? A Jewish Lesbian From Paradise. "You oughtta be in pictures," I said, and blew myself a kiss.

A Sorry State
(for my friends in Oregon and Colorado)

The backlash felt like whiplash: an unexpected, out-of-the-blue, unbe-
lievably painful jolt that burst open our eyes, snapped our heads around
and sent us into a high speed tailspin, whirling us around and around
until dazed, we stopped, shook our heads, took a deep breath and headed
slowly down the long, long road before us.....

Amanda Edwards was running out of patience. She had to get to
work on time today, and as she poured Megan's Ninja Turtle cereal
into her Bert and Ernie bowl, she wondered for the millionth time
why Adam couldn't take the child to day care once in a while. Not
every day, as some wives insisted, or even every other day. Just on days
like today when she had the biggest presentation of her whole career
scheduled in front of the entire board. But Adam wouldn't hear of it.
God forbid *he* should arrive at the office with tears and snot dripping
down the front of *his* freshly pressed suit. It worried Amanda that
Megan still cried every time she got dropped off; though Jackie, her
teacher had assured her dozens of times that it was a normal part of
the "morning transition." And Megan was usually fine even before
Amanda pulled out of the center's driveway. Jackie would whirl her
around until she elicited a giggle or two, and then lure Megan inside
with just the right toy; a yellow truck, a stuffed penguin, a puzzle of
two fuzzy-looking bears. Sometimes Amanda thought Jackie knew her
daughter better than she did, but no matter; that's what the woman
was being paid for.

65

"C'mon, Megan, let's go honey." Amanda grabbed her briefcase and handed Megan her ladybug knapsack. She buckled the child into her car seat and headed out, reminding herself to re-negotiate their morning routine with Adam. Plenty of other fathers dropped their kids off, she thought as she drove, noticing the rush hour traffic was unusually light this morning: a blessing. Maybe she'd talk to Adam after dinner tonight. There hadn't been any time that morning. In fact, Amanda mused, I don't even remember seeing Adam this morning. Not that that was unusual. Vaguely she remembered a peck on the cheek and a shadow in the doorway, long before the alarm on her side of the bed jarred her awake. Typical, Amanda thought. That's what you get for marrying someone who's just as much a workaholic as you.

"C'mon, honey, let's go find Jackie." Amanda unbuckled Megan who ran to the front yard of the day care center and then stopped. A new woman was waiting out front. Christ, a substitute on today of all days? Amanda sighed and knelt down, praying that her pantyhose wouldn't run. "Megan, Jackie's not here today. This lady will take care of you and I'm sure Jackie will be back tomorrow."

"Uh...not quite," the woman said.

"What?" Amanda stood up, keeping one arm around Megan's shoulders.

"Jackie's gone," the woman said.

"Gone?" Amanda echoed.

"You heard about the new law, banishing gays and lesbians from the state? Well, uh, Jackie left this morning."

"Jackie left?" Amanda repeated, not really listening to the rest of what was being said. "Well, what's your name?"

"Susanne."

"Amanda, honey, this is Susanne and she'll be your new teacher."

"Uh...not quite," the woman said again. "We're running on half staff here, so we can only take half the children. State law: teacher/child ratio can't be more than one to four. I'm afraid we're all full."

"What?" Amanda's voice came out in a squeak. "But I have to get to work today. I have an extremely important meeting. And I'm paid up for the entire month!"

"Sorry." Susanne shrugged and went off to greet another unsuspecting parent and child.

"Christ." Amanda shook her head and reached down for her daughter's hand. "C'mon, Megan, we're going to Grandma's." Luckily, Amanda's mother had no plans for the day and was delighted to take her granddaughter. "Mommy will be back at six o'clock." Amanda raced back into the car and tore to the office.

"Bill, sorry I'm late," Amanda announced as she flew into the conference room. But the room was empty. Strange, Amanda thought, heading for Bill's office. She found her boss sitting at his desk with his head in his hands.

"Bill, are you all right?" Amanda tapped his shoulder. "What happened to the meeting?"

"Oh, Amanda." Bill shook his head like he was trying to wake up. "It's unbelievable. Overnight half the sales force is gone. Gone. Not to mention the reps, the accountants, the department heads, Christ, even the VP. How am I supposed to run a company?"

"Bill, what are you talking about?" Amanda wondered if her boss was having a nervous breakdown. He wouldn't be the first to crack under such pressure.

"Amanda, don't you read the papers? They passed that law, you know, making homosexuality illegal, and banning all homosexuals from the state. Half this company is gone. Gone. When you didn't show up this morning, I was beginning to wonder."

"Oh, Bill, don't be ridiculous. Megan had a day care crisis." She thrust her hands on her hips. "Do you want to go over my notes for the meeting?"

"What good are they? What's the use?" Bill ran his fingers through his hair. "I'm all washed up. Finished."

"Bill, we can handle this. No one's irreplaceable. Let's just..."

"Amanda, the office is closed today. Just go home."

"But Bill," Amanda snapped open her briefcase. "I've been working on these reports for more than a month. I don't think..."

"Take a day off, Amanda." Bill's voice was firm. "I can't run a ship without a crew."

"Shit." Amanda took her things and clicked down the hallway into her own office. She buzzed her secretary but got no answer. "A whole month of work for nothing." She sat down at her desk and then stood up again. "Oh, the hell with it. Bill said take a day off, I'm taking a day off."

Amanda got back into her car and started it, not sure where she was heading. Of course I could take Megan off my mother's hands, she thought, but quickly dismissed the idea. When was the last time I had an entire day to myself, Amanda wondered. No work, no Adam, no Megan, just *moi*. What a concept. Amanda turned on the radio and started to hum as she pulled out of the parking lot. I'm going to have some fun today, she thought, heading for the mall. First I'll get my hair done, and a manicure, then a little shopping, lunch at the coffee shop where they have those wonderful Greek pastries....hell, I could even get used to this.

Amanda parked and pulled open the door to Hair's To You. "Hi, Donna," she said to the receptionist. "I know I don't have an appointment today, but do you think Brian can squeeze me in? I'm pretty flexible, I have the day off. Whenever he has an opening."

"Brian's gone, honey." Donna's voice was thick from crying and she looked up at Amanda with red, mascara-streaked eyes.

"Gone?"

"He left this morning."

"Why?"

"Why? Because the people in this stupid state voted to remove him and *his kind*, that's why." Donna spit out each word.

"His kind? What are you talking about?"

"You knew Brian was gay, Amanda, didn't you?"

"Brian?" Amanda's voice rose an octave. "But he was so sweet! And...and he flirted with me! I thought he was a lady's man."

Donna laughed and then her eyes filled. "Brian flirted with anything that moved, and a few things that didn't." She sighed and looked at her appointment book. "I really can't squeeze you in today, Amanda. Everyone's double-booked with Brian's appointments."

"That's okay." Amanda waved her hand in front of her face, as though she was trying to clear something away. Brian, a homosexual? Brian, whose magic hands shampooed all her cares away and then styled her hair so meticulously that she always felt beautiful when she left the salon? Sometimes Amanda even joked with her friends that an appointment with Brian was better than having sex, and more often than she'd care to admit, Amanda had in fact imagined what sleeping with Brian would be like. If he could make just the top of her head feel so loved with his strong, capable fingers....Amanda's throat tightened and she felt slightly sick.

"Are you all right, honey?" Donna's voice broke into Amanda's thoughts.

"Yes, I'm fine," she said, briskly.

"Do you want to sign this petition?" Donna waved a clipboard in front of her face.

"Uh, I'll think about it." Amanda never signed anything. Too dangerous. The next thing you know, the FBI, the CIA or the IRS was at your door. "I'll call you next week for an appointment, Donna." Amanda walked briskly through the salon and out the back door, into the mall.

Lots of stores in the mall were closed, and those that were open were obviously understaffed. As the morning wore on, lines at the cash registers grew longer and longer, and shoppers grew more and more impatient. Amanda waited half an hour at Filene's to pay for a blue silk scarf, and she couldn't find anyone at the gourmet coffee shop where she liked to buy her imported tea. Her favorite florist was shut down (the sign in the window said, WILL RETURN WHEN HELL FREEZES OVER) and the one salesclerk at the bookstore where Amanda loved to browse had her hands more than full as she tried to keep order at her cash register. Amanda actually noticed two teenagers in the back of the store sneaking books into their backpacks, and she left in a hurry, her heart thumping in her chest. What next, she wondered, looters and riots like L.A.?

Amanda headed back to her car and drove home. She needed gas, but the line was so long, and the attendant so obviously frazzled, that she changed her mind and moved on. She stopped at the grocery store on the corner for some half-and-half for her coffee. Again, the store was obviously working with half its staff or less, but Amanda waited it out. "Unbelievable," she said to no one in particular as she stood in line. "What's going on here? Did homosexuals run this entire town?"

"My dentist was one, can you believe it?" The woman in front of Amanda turned around. "I was supposed to have a root canal done this morning. Do you have any idea how hard it is to find a good dentist?"

"You think you got problems?" Amanda turned to see the woman behind her posed with a head of broccoli in mid air. "My real estate broker is gone. Gone, right in the middle of selling our house. What are we supposed to do? We've already bought another place. My husband said we should sue, so I called our lawyer and guess what? He's gone, too."

"What is wrong with you people?" A young woman in the next line over gestured with a carton of yogurt. "All you think about is yourself. These are human beings we're talking about here, who had to leave their homes, their jobs...."

"I say good riddance," a man behind her jumped in. "Now we'll stop AIDS and child abuse."

"Oh, please," the woman with the yogurt groaned.

"They should have seen it coming," the woman in front of Amanda said. "This bill's been around for months. They should have left when they had plenty of time."

"No one believed that it would pass," the young woman said, quietly. "We didn't want to believe it. We were in too much denial, like the Jews in Nazi Germany."

"How dare you compare this to that?" a man shouted. "My father died in those death camps..."

"They only got what they deserved."

"Who, the Jews?" The man's fist was raised.

"No, the queers."

"They make me sick. I'm glad they're gone."

"Bunch of commie dykes."

"Shut up! You're all a bunch of intolerant, ignorant, bigoted morons," the young woman shouted.

"She must be one of them!" Someone grabbed the woman's arms and her yogurt crashed to the ground with a splat. "Call the authorities. Get the police!"

"Let me go! Let me go!" The woman struggled and Amanda watched, horrified as two men in uniform arrived out of nowhere it seemed, and took her away. Suddenly, Amanda couldn't stand being there a minute longer. She ran outside, dropping her cream in her haste and drove home in a daze. Had everyone gone mad? She went inside the house and locked the door behind her.

Safely cushioned from the rest of the world, Amanda made herself a cup of black coffee and just stared at it. What a strange day. I should call Bill at the office, she thought, bringing the phone over to the kitchen table, and giving in to her workaholic tendencies. But somehow, lifting her fingers to dial the number seemed too much of an effort. She could call Adam of course, but he hated being interrupted at work. He always called her at the office at two o'clock sharp when he got back from lunch to check in, see what was for dinner, and chitchat in that boring, husband-wife way that they swore they would never fall into: "Did you pick up my shirts from the cleaners?" "Did you remember it's parents' night at Megan's daycare center?" Even though Amanda found the endless, mundane details of their life hopelessly trivial and annoying, there was a comfort to it all as well, a comfort she longed for, especially today when the whole world around her was going to hell in a handbasket. But it was only a little after one o'clock; she had a whole hour to wait. And even if she decided to risk Adam's annoyance and call him, she wouldn't find him in. He took his lunch from twelve-thirty until two o'clock every day. He was so predictable, Amanda could set her clock by him.

Amanda carried the phone into the living room and turned on the TV to wait for Adam's call. Of course he'd call her at home when he realized she wasn't at work. God only knew what was going on at his office. Amanda flicked through the channels to pass the time and then laughed at herself. Who would ever have imagined me, sitting by the phone in the middle of a workday waiting for my husband to call like a starry-eyed teenager, she thought as she settled into the recliner with her lukewarm cup of coffee and the remote control. The news was on and Amanda watched, fascinated, as microphones were shoved into face after tearful face. "My son is gone. I didn't even know he was gay." "My daughter left early this morning. I helped her and her lover pack." "My boss shut the shop down. I never dreamed this would put me out of work." "My uncle's knee operation had to be postponed until they can find another specialist." Amanda flipped through the TV channels, but it was all the same: interviews with bewildered and bereft parents, siblings, co-workers, even a woman who, between sobs, voiced concern over her grandmother who had been forced to leave. And of course, to balance out the news, the reporters had to interview people who were glad to be rid of "those animals," as one man put it. But even he had to admit he was amazed at the sheer number of people this turn of events was affecting.

The news ended with a reporter urging people to stay inside unless it was absolutely necessary, because as night fell, there was sure to be violence. With so many stores understaffed or deserted, the looters were sure to be out in full force once the curtain of darkness descended. The National Guard was already on its way.

As Amanda stared at the TV screen in disbelief, the phone rang, making her jump. Exactly two o'clock, right on schedule. At least some things in this world could still be counted on. "Adam," she cried into the receiver. "Do you believe all this madness? I had to take Megan to my mother's this morning, and Bill sent me home and..."

"Amanda, listen," Adam interrupted her. "I can't talk long, there's a line waiting for the phone..."

"A line? Everything is so crazy! Where are you?"

"I'm just over the state border. Listen, Amanda, I didn't want to have to tell you this way, but there's nothing I can do about that. Maybe it's better like this anyway, so I don't have to live a lie anymore. Don't think I didn't love you, Amanda because I did, and Megan, too, my God, she's everything to me, but this was just always inside me and..."

"Adam, what are you talking about?"

"Amanda, I'm in love with Jeffrey, you know from my office. It's only been going on for a few months, but in my heart I know it's right. I was going to get up the courage to tell you somehow, but then this happened...."

"What time will you be home for supper?" Amanda asked, taking the cordless phone back into the kitchen. She opened the freezer door. "If I take the pork chops out now, I think they'll be defrosted by tonight."

"Amanda, listen to me. I won't be coming home for supper. I can't. I'll call you tomorrow when things aren't so crazy."

"Did you call the garage about my car, Adam? It's still making that funny noise when I shift...."

"Amanda, please. Forget about the car. I'm trying to tell you something. I'm gay. I'm a homosexual. I'm in love with Jeffrey Bloom. I am not coming home."

Oh my God. By the time Amanda's brain finally registered her husband's words, the line had gone dead. "Adam?" she whispered, dropping the phone to the floor. "Adam?" Amanda half sat/half fell down into a chair. Her Adam was gay? Her husband was a homosexual? Quickly her mind flew back to the last time they had had sex, but frankly she couldn't remember when that was. Well, she had Megan, didn't she? And that must prove something, though Amanda wasn't quite sure what. Suddenly she wanted her daughter there with her more than anything. She snatched up her car keys and then froze. What was she supposed to tell her mother? And everyone else for that matter? How was she supposed to pay the mortgage? Who was she supposed to snuggle up to at night? Who *had* she been snuggling up to? Her Adam, predictable as the sun coming up in the morning and setting at night, with his daily two o'clock phone calls, his Monday night game of tennis, his goodnight kiss on her cheek every single night at eleven-thirty sharp right when the *Tonight Show* came on, her Adam was gay? Amanda grabbed her pocketbook off the kitchen table and almost made it to the front door before her knees gave way and she collapsed in the front hallway into a dead faint.

All over the state people were discovering what we've known all along; that everyone has gay men and lesbians in their lives. But no matter. Across the state line, there were delighted cries of, "You?" "You?" "No, I don't believe it. You?" "You? I always wondered." "Oh my God, you?" And our tears and rage and terror gave way to joy momentarily when someone's car radio blared "I Am What I Am" followed by "We Are Family" as we embraced each other and danced in unbelievably strong numbers before we marched forward, strong, proud and determined to survive.

Let Me Explain

Let me explain a few things about Stevie and about myself. I know you think you knew him best, Ray, and I'm sure there are things you know about him that I don't know and wouldn't want to know, believe me. But Ray, don't forget, I knew Stevie for the first eighteen years of his life, before you ever laid eyes on him. And believe me, there are things about a person nobody in the world except their own mother knows.

He was a beautiful baby, and a good baby. He had huge, dark chocolate eyes, with long, long lashes, eyelashes any girl would kill for. I used to joke that by the time he was two, his eyelashes would be down to his knees. And he had gorgeous hair, full, thick black curls from the day he was born. He got that from his father's side of the family, not that the bum stuck around long enough to see what his own flesh and blood looked like. It was just Stevie and me against the world from day one. I didn't mind so much though because Stevie was an angel. He hardly cried and he slept through the night which was a blessing, believe me, because I had to get up very early and drop him off at my mother's before I went to work in the morning.

He was a good boy, normal in every way. He loved cars, trucks, buses, anything that moved. He never played with dolls or wanted to try on my clothes or anything. He was normal. He even liked sports, especially swimming. He was like a little fish, always in the water. He made the varsity swim team when he was only in the tenth grade. I used to go to his swim meets whenever I could, sitting up in the bleachers, choking on that thick, chlorine air. I tried to be both mother and father to him, but I couldn't always be there. Sometimes I think that was the problem; other times I think maybe I was there too much. You know what they say about mama's boys, I'm sure.

Stevie loved art, too. Drawing, painting, clay. He used to sketch me after dinner when I was reading the paper with my feet up. He was no Rembrandt, that's for sure, but he could get a pretty good likeness. I don't think he ever wanted to be world famous or anything. He thought a lot about teaching and during his senior year he volunteered in a fifth grade art class once a week. One day, he told me, he's walking around the room looking at all the kids' art work and he sees a boy's written "F—k Mr. D'Amato" on his paper with bright orange poster paint.

"That's not art," Stevie says, and he folds the kid's painting in half. Then he unfolds it and the paper now has a big blob on it like a Rorschach test. "Now that's art," says Stevie. By the end of the year, the kids had all signed a petition asking the principal to fire Mr. D'Amato and hire Stevie in his place. Stevie wouldn't let them show it to the principal; he didn't want Mr. D'Amato's feelings to be hurt, he's just that kind of person, you know, sensitive. But he did bring that petition home to hang up on the wall. It made him so proud.

Stevie didn't have a girlfriend in high school, but he had a lot of girl friends, you know, friends that are girls. There was one in particular, Lori I think her name was, that he was very close to, but nothing came of it. I didn't worry about it though; no one marries their high school sweetheart anymore. I figured Stevie was just a late bloomer and he'd meet someone in college.

I wanted Stevie to stay here in New Jersey, but he only wanted to go to San Francisco. "Ma, a city right on the water," he kept saying. I told him New York was right on the water, too, and there were plenty of art schools in Manhattan, but he had his heart set on California and I never could say no to him. My parents offered to help out so off he went to college, three-thousand miles away, my baby. I suppose it was time for him to leave, time for both of us really to have lives of our own. Before he left he gave me a beautiful white mug that he made himself on the pottery wheel at school. He put a big heart on it and around the rim he'd painted the words "I love you, Mom," with a shiny blue glaze. It's funny, now that I think of it, it's like he knew he'd never be back. But that never occurred to me then. I was so touched that he made that mug for me, I still drink my coffee out of it every morning. It's nice and big, definitely a mug, not a cup, and it's comforting to hold between my hands.

I'll never forget that first winter vacation when Stevie came home to visit. The four months he'd been away seemed like forever. I couldn't wait to see him, but when I picked him up at the airport, I hardly recognized him. It wasn't just the crazy haircut with one side all sticking up, or the silver loop in his ear that almost gave his grandfather a heart attack. No, it was something else. Stevie walked different, he talked different, he ate different... I kept my eye on him and suddenly one day I knew. He's got a girl, I thought to myself. My Stevie's not a virgin anymore. That's what's different. That's what's giving him this confidence.

So after supper the last night of his visit, I asked him. We always did the dishes together; Stevie washed, I dried and we talked. So I said to him, "Okay, Stevie, who is she?" and he said, "Who's who, Ma?" and I said, "You've got a girl. C'mon, it's written all over your face."

He handed me a glass to dry and said the two words no parent ever wants to hear: "I'm gay." He said it so matter-of-factly, like "I'm hungry," or "I'm tired." And he kept scrubbing at this blob of tomato sauce on the white dinner plate he was washing without skipping a beat. I almost dropped the glass he had just handed me, but that would have been too dramatic. I didn't know what to say, so I just said "Are you sure?" and he said, "Ma, I'm positive," and I'll never forget that, Ray, because a year later Stevie called me up and said those exact same words, "Ma, I'm positive." I didn't know what he was talking about. "Ma, I'm positive," he repeated. "HIV positive." Then softer, "Ma, I have AIDS."

Ray, you have no idea what a mother goes through with something like this. I sat down, no I fell down into a kitchen chair and all my blood rushed to my feet. I thought I was going to pass out, but I didn't. Again I asked, "Are you sure?" and again he said, "I'm positive."

My mind raced: *are you sure you're positive? I'm sure I'm positive. Are you positive you're positive? I'm positive I'm positive. Are you absolutely positive? I'm absolutely positive. Positively positive? Positively positive.*

I forced my mind to come back to the phone, to listen to what he was saying. Something about AZT, DDI, KS, PCP. I heard the words but I wasn't really listening. I didn't know what any of those letters stood for and I really didn't care. I was a million miles away, remembering my little Stevie sitting at the kitchen table with a bowl of alphabet soup in front of him saying, "D is for doggie, S is for Stevie, M is for Mommy," waving his big spoon in the air.

I asked him if he wanted me to come, but he said no, he felt fine. I asked him if he wanted to come home but again he said no, he wanted to keep going to school for as long as he could. For as long as he could...those words went right through my heart like a knife, Ray. After I hung up the phone I started to cry and I didn't stop for weeks. For weeks I cried. I went over our lives with a fine-tooth comb: what did I do wrong, what sins could I have possibly committed in this life or any other to bring so much pain onto my son, my only son? I spoke to him every week and he kept telling me he was fine, I shouldn't worry about him, I should take care of myself. See, that's the kind of person he is. He even sent me a phone number for some support group for mothers of gay sons or something, but I never called. I'm just not that type of person, Ray. I've always been independent; I'm sure you know Stevie is, too.

Stevie didn't come home his next winter vacation—he was doing some sort of independent study—and at the end of the spring semester he decided he wanted to stay in San Francisco for the summer. I asked him again if he wanted me to come and again he said no, he was fine.

"Are you sure, Stevie?" I asked.

"I'm positive," he said, and then he must have realized the double entendre of his answer because he added, "Don't worry, Ma. PWA's can live a long, long time."

Again with the letters. "Who?"

"People with AIDS." Silence. "Don't worry, Ma. Ray's really great.

He takes good care of me."

My heart clutched. "Who?"

"Ray. My lover."

That word. Why couldn't he say my roommate, or my friend? Who was this child of mine, this stranger who took a man to be his lover? I felt like I didn't know my own son anymore.

"You don't need to come, Ma," Stevie said again one August morning during one of our weekly calls. "I'm fine." And even though his voice sounded weak, I believed him. Stevie never was a morning person, I reminded myself. If I would have only used my head, I'd have known he was protecting me like he always did. Even when he was a kid, Stevie wouldn't show me his cut finger, his scraped knee. He didn't want to be a bother; he hated when I fussed and worried over him. "Ma, it's nothing," he'd say. He didn't want me to take care of him, he only wanted to take care of me. "Ma, sit down," he'd say when I got home from work. "I'll make supper." So good, so good he was.

Of course I should have known he wasn't fine, Ray. I should have jumped on a plane that very day, that very minute, but Ray you don't understand, you can't possibly know what it was like for me. I wanted to believe he was fine. I needed to believe it. I'd only had a year to digest the fact that I'd never dance at my son's wedding, I'd never bump hips with my daughter-in-law in the kitchen over pots and pans. One year, Ray, to accept that no one would ever call me grandma, there wouldn't be any plump cherubs with cheeks to pinch. I couldn't take any more bad news. I'm sure you think I was being selfish, Ray, but I'm only human after all. Who plans on having a gay son? Not me, that's for sure. And on top of that, my boy was sick, sick with a disease I knew nothing about. Who wouldn't want to believe those two magic words, "I'm fine"? I believed him all right, For months I believed him every Sunday morning. "I'm fine, Ma, really. I'm fine."

And then came that terrible Sunday when I picked up the phone and heard your unfamiliar deep voice. "This is Ray," you said, and when it was obvious your name didn't register, you repeated it: "Ray, you know. Steven's lover." Again that word. And how strange to hear you call him *Steven*. It sounded so grown-up and intimate. "Steven's been asking for you," you said. "I think you should come."

So I flew out to San Francisco and you picked me up at the airport. I have to say I was fully prepared to hate you, Ray, but I just couldn't. You were so young and there was so much pain in your eyes. And when you took my bag so politely, all of a sudden I knew you had a mother somewhere, you were somebody's child, too.

We didn't say much on the way to your house and after you parked, you waited for a minute before you got out of the car. "He doesn't look very good," you said, trying to prepare me. "He's very thin and he probably won't get out of bed."

"I understand," I said, but of course I didn't. You can't possibly be talking about my son, I thought, as I followed you up the steps.

Your house was very clean and Stevie's drawings were all over the walls. I looked at them while you went into the bedroom to see if he was awake. A minute later you motioned to me.

"I'll leave you two alone," you said and disappeared. I took two steps into the room and my blood stopped cold. I absolutely froze. I looked at my son, my beautiful son, and all I could see were his two dark eyes, enormous in what used to be his face.

"Stevie," I said at the same instant his mouth formed the word, "Ma." Neither of us moved until tears began to flow out of his left eye and trickle down his cheek. Then somehow I managed to lift my feet, though they felt like wet cement, and drag myself over to sit on the edge of his bed and wipe his tears with the back of my hand.

I will never forget the sight of my baby lying there as long as I live. He was nothing but a bag of bones. He looked like those pictures you see of people at Auschwitz. So thin, so thin. And all his hair gone, those thick, beautiful curls. Even his eyelashes.

Oh Stevie, bone of my bone, blood of my blood, why didn't you let me know, why didn't you come home so I could take care of you like only a mother can? Why didn't you tell me how sick you really were? I know what you're thinking, Ray, why didn't I ask? But I did ask, and he kept saying he was fine. Yes, his voice sounded weak, but I had no idea. I didn't ask my son to move three-thousand miles away and start a new life, a life that had no room for me. I had no idea what

AIDS could do to a person, how quickly he would become ill, how fast he would deteriorate.

I sat with him all afternoon. We didn't say much. I held his hand and stroked his arm, such a thin arm, like a pencil it was, my poor Stevie who used to be so proud of his muscles a million years ago when he was the number one breast stroke swimmer on the varsity team. We watched TV, or Stevie watched and I pretended to. He'd doze off every now and then and I'd gaze at his gaunt face while he slept. He had small, red sores on his chin and cheeks; later he told me he had them inside his mouth too, and it hurt him to eat. Oh Stevie, flesh of my flesh, I would chew your food for you like a mama bird, I would gladly exchange your frail body for my own.

At six o'clock Stevie's watch beeped, startling him awake. He hoisted himself up and said, "Meds, Ma. You better not watch." Still protecting me, even now. He took a blue pill, a yellow pill, a red pill, and then he gave himself an injection in his belly, the only part of his entire body that still boasted flesh.

Then you came in, Ray, to check on us and see about dinner, and when I saw Stevie's eyes light up at the sight of your face, at last, for one moment I understood something. I saw that you were two people who loved each other, nothing more and nothing less. And when you helped Stevie out of bed so he could lean on you and inch his way down the hall to the bathroom like he was ninety years old instead of twenty, I saw how carefully, how tenderly, how lovingly you support-ed him. And just for that one moment my heart ached not only for myself.

When you brought Stevie back to bed, I was shocked all over again at the sight of him. Not that he'd changed in the ten minutes you were gone, Ray, but in a funny way I was growing used to what he looked like. I read somewhere that happened in the concentration camps, too. People were so used to seeing each other looking like walking, talking skeletons, that it seemed normal. It's amazing what a human being can get used to, isn't it? While you were helping Stevie, I got up to stretch a little, and I saw a picture on the dresser; you and Stevie on top of a mountain somewhere. He was smiling right into the camera, his cheeks flushed, his hair blowing off his face.

"That's from a hike we took in the Sierra Nevadas," you said, coming back into the room. I turned around, expecting to see the laughing boy in the photograph, but instead I saw my baby, weightless in your arms being gently lowered onto the bed.

"I called out for pizza," you said and all three of us waited on the bed for it to come. "I was macrobiotic," Stevie said, his words pronounced slowly and with great effort, "but now I eat whatever I want, to try to get some calories." I nodded, numb. We ate the pizza out of the box and I saw how hard it was for Stevie to eat, one piece was all he could manage and that took him the better part of an hour. Afterwards he looked at his watch and said, again with effort, "Ma, did I take my pills?"

"Yes, Stevie," I said, and turned away so he couldn't see my tears. All I could think of was my father driving my mother crazy every few hours: "Edna, did I take my heart pill today?" Stevie was too young for this, too young too young.

"Don't cry, Ma," he said, and I turned back to him. "I've had an okay life."

"Stevie, you're going to get better," I said, not bothering to hide my tears. "You're not going to die."

"I am going to die, Ma," he said, his words slow and gentle, like he was the parent and I was the child. "It's okay. I'm not bitter or angry anymore. I'm not even scared. AIDS is affecting everyone on the planet and this is how it's affecting me."

Don't, I wanted to scream. Don't accept it, Stevie. Don't give up. Don't stop fighting. But he was so very tired. His short speech had totally exhausted him. I could see he was ready to die, that it would in fact be a blessing to put an end to his suffering.

So, when you called me at my hotel four nights later, Ray, I knew. It was three o'clock in the morning but I wasn't sleeping. I had just woken up from a dream: I was back home sitting at my own kitchen table, drinking coffee out of the mug Stevie made me, when all of a sudden the mug disintegrated in my hands. It didn't drop or crack or shatter. It was just gone. Half a minute later the phone rang, and you didn't have to say a word, Ray. I knew.

I didn't speak to anyone at the funeral. All those young men in their tight jeans and white shirts, walking by slowly with tears in their eyes... any one of them could have been Stevie. And how I wished one of them was Stevie, and someone else's son was lying in that coffin. It's a terrible thing to wish, Ray, but who can blame me? I know this is hard for you, but you must understand that for a mother to lose her son, her only child, is the worst thing in the world. I would have gladly lain down in that coffin if it meant Stevie could get up and walk away. Gladly.

And now you write to me, something about a panel for a quilt you're making in memory of Stevie. The AIDS quilt, you called it. You want something from me to put on it, you say, you know it would mean a lot to him, you know that's what Stevie would want.

I want to know how you know what Stevie wants, Ray. Do you know how to speak to the dead? Because if you do, tell Stevie how much I love him, how much I miss him. Tell him I think about him every day and I dream about him every night. He's never sick in my dreams, Ray, he's always healthy: sitting in his high chair, stuffing fistfuls of spaghetti into his mouth; sprawled across the living room floor, his head bent over a drawing; in his bathing suit at a swim meet ready to dive into the water, his toes curled over the edge of the pool.

It's the same thing every night. Every night I go to sleep, I dream about Stevie, I wake up crying at three o'clock, the same time you called, Ray, to say Stevie's life was over. I want you to know that from that moment on, my life was over, too.

So today I go to my mailbox and find the letter from you. I was more than a little surprised; frankly I never thought I'd see or hear from you again, and to tell you the truth, that was fine with me. I don't know if you can understand that, Ray. I don't know if this explains anything. I did my best and I know you did, too. I know you loved Stevie; I saw the way you looked at him, it was right there in your eyes.

I hope this quilt you're making helps you in some way, I hope it makes you feel better somehow. Thank you for writing to me and inviting me to be a part of it, but Ray, nothing in this entire world could possibly comfort me now. My life is over. And that's why I'm contributing to Stevie's quilt panel what you'll find inside this box: the two jagged pieces of my bruised and broken heart.

PART III: LEAN MEAN SEX MACHINE

Lilly Valentine

She stood in front of me at the check out line of Stop And Shop, her hand hovering over the can of cat food and the pint of cream she was buying. I loaded my groceries onto the conveyor belt behind hers, trying to remain calm, trying to remember to keep breathing. She smelled like lilacs and her sweater was on inside out, which would have been merely sloppy on anyone else, but only made her look impossibly sexy, especially the way it drooped off one shoulder in a flashdance kind of fashion. I was a goner. She wore a short skirt and sandals, and a mile of shiny black hair floated straight down her back. I couldn't see her face but it didn't matter. I prayed for the cash register to break or the tape to run out, anything to give me a minute to think. How could I start a conversation without sounding like an idiot? *Nice morning, isn't it? Do you come here often? Do you always drink half-and-half with your Nine Lives?*

Hell, she could be straight, married even, but God knows that had never stopped me before. The hand that now rested lightly on the can of cat food was soft looking; the nails filed into delicate pink and white ovals, the fourth finger ringless as all the others.

The cashier started the conveyor belt moving and rang up her purchases. As she took two dollar bills from her wallet I caught a glimpse of her profile—just a glimpse, mind you—but that was enough to set my heart thunking in my chest. Her eye met mine for the briefest of seconds and a tiny smile flickered across her lips before she turned away and her hair fell between us like the curtain at the end of a play. Had I been so obvious? Was her smile an invitation? Or was the fact that she had turned away a dismissal? Hard to tell, but no matter, for she picked up her small shopping bag and proceeded toward the door and out of my life forever without once looking back.

Ah well, easy come, easy go, I told myself, watching her graceful departure. She probably had someone waiting at home with the coffee brewing and the Sunday paper spread all over the kitchen table. Someone who didn't want her to get out of bed at all, but she had to, for the kitten's meowing was driving her crazy and damn, she was all out of cat food. Oh, all right honey, but hurry back and while you're at it, could you pick up some cream? Or then again, maybe she was all alone, woman and cat in a fourth floor walk up, and this was their solitary weekend treat. But I highly doubted it; a woman of her charms couldn't possibly be alone on a Sunday morning.

"Is this yours?" The cashier broke into my thoughts, holding a wallet toward me.

"No," I replied.

"It must be that woman's," the cashier said, looking toward the exit "Damn."

"I'll give it to her," I said, hardly believing my good luck. I took my bag of groceries out to the parking lot, but there was no sign of her. Not to worry, I told myself as I drove home. Now I had an excuse to call her, or better yet to drop by in person to return the wallet to its rightful owner. But perhaps a phone call would be better, for in all likelihood she wasn't alone. She did have that morning-after-the-night-before look with her inside out sweater and all. Then again, any decent lover would have accompanied her to the market, or better yet left her at home and gone to pick up the supplies while she lounged about in bed, the morning sun bathing her glorious body in swimming stripes through the venetian blinds. Yes, that's what any decent person would have done, I thought as I carried my bundles into the house. She should get rid of the jerk, I decided. Obviously she needs a new lover. Someone more compassionate, kinder, more loving. Someone, for example, like me.

I unpacked my food and then sat down with her wallet like a much anticipated dessert, my mouth practically watering. First I checked the cash; a few singles and a five spot. Then I looked through her cards: a Sears charge, an automatic bank card, a membership to the Y. Her name was Lilly Valentine. That knocked me out. A woman born for romance. Hearts and flowers all the way. I had to take the chance to meet her, ask her out, maybe even wrap us both up in all that luscious hair like a black silk blanket. Fate had thrown us together once and I had missed my cue by not speaking. But persistent fate was kind enough to give me a second chance: wasn't the wallet I was holding in my hand proof?

I dug around some more and at last came up with what I was looking for. Her license. The address on the back was not far from my home, a half hour's drive, forty minutes at the most. I held the license in my palm for a moment before I turned it over, imagining her lovely face smiling up at me. Everyone looks terrible on their license photo, but even a terrible photo of Lilly Valentine would surely be more stunning than most. Still, nothing prepared me for what I was about to see.

I turned the license over and gasped out loud, drawing it up to my face for a closer look. And then I pushed the license away, recoiling as though I'd been slapped.

The right side of Lilly Valentine's face was crumpled as an old paper bag someone had packed their lunch in a thousand years ago. Her eye was squashed shut and her lip was permanently curled down. Her skin was a reddish-purple, halfway between an eggplant and the inside of a blood orange. The left side of her face was perfect, in every sense of the word. Creamy skin, almond-shaped eyes, full lips; exactly the kind of face you would expect to belong to a woman named Lilly Valentine. I put my finger over the right side of her face and stared at her beauty. Then I covered her left side and stared at her misfortune. What had happened to Lilly Valentine? Had she been trapped in a burning building? Marred by a jealous lover? Hurt in an automobile accident? Scarred in the birth canal?

I knew that I would never know. For instead of looking her up in the phone book, or arriving on her doorstep with her wallet in one hand and a stem of lilies in the other, I merely put her possession in a padded envelope and mailed it away without so much as a note, for what could I possibly say? It was my loss for sure, not hers, for I certainly was not in any way worthy of her friendship, let alone anything more. Clearly she deserves a much better specimen of the human race than I with which to spend her days. I wondered if Lilly Valentine had left her wallet behind as some sort of test: surely she had felt the heat of my interest pulsing between us at the supermarket, surely she had read something in that briefest of seconds when we had seen eye to eye. Perhaps she had learned to protect herself from jerks like me in this manner, for I could only imagine how many times she had been hurt before. If it was a test I had failed, and failed miserably. For even though I felt compassion when I looked at her face, as well as pity and some form of love, I knew that my desire for Lilly Valentine had evaporated the instant I looked at her photo, as surely as it had sprung to life the minute I'd spotted her on the check out line. And to this day, I am truly and thoroughly ashamed.

The AB Spot

I think it was big of me to come. Some would say it was big of her to invite me. It doesn't really matter, I suppose. What matters is there I was, standing in borrowed high heels next to her Great Aunt Mildred whose perfume surrounded me like a cloud of pink smog, and there she was, all gowned and veiled, standing under the chuppah with her back to us all, ready to tie the knot for the rest of her life.

All sorts of thoughts were wandering through my mind, as you can imagine, but the one that stuck, for some reason, was the AB spot. You've heard of the infamous G spot, haven't you? Well, the AB spot is the same, only different.

I discovered it one day, early on in our relationship when we were lying in bed one afternoon (oh, young love!) and she was kvetching about her boss, who had given her a hard time about taking the day off so she could spend it with me. Which wasn't what she told him of course. She'd said she had some family matters to take care of, but still, he'd threatened her with all kinds of ridiculous things even though she got one personal day a month (despite her shmuck of a boss, it was a pretty cushy job). She went on and on and though I was listening, I was also quite distracted by the texture of her golden skin lying right beside me.

"Do you know you have a beauty mark under your ear?" I finally interrupted her.

"Where?" She stopped her tirade and felt the side of her cheek with her finger.

"No, not there. In the corner, right where your jaw meets your

91

neck. Here." I kissed it.

"I never knew that," she said, feeling around with her finger. "Kiss it again."

I did. "All better now?" I asked.

"Yes," she said, snuggling down into me so that we could commence with what we'd taken the day off to do. Ever since then, that particular beauty mark (for there were others to be discovered) was known as the All Better, or AB Spot, which I would kiss whenever necessary to make things all better. Sometimes it worked splendidly, and sometimes it didn't work at all, especially toward the end of our relationship, which was a mere year and seven months ago.

I sighed deeply and looked up at the bima. I wondered if *he* knew about the AB spot. It was time, the inevitable you-may-kiss-the-bride time, and I watched them turn toward each other: he, holding her face between his hands like a precious cut-glass bowl, and she, looking up at him with eyes of pure, liquid love. As he drew her closer, I watched the pinky of his left hand search and then settle firmly under the delicious lobe of her ear, and I knew that he knew. But she looked so utterly exquisite, I couldn't hate her. Him, yes, certainly and forever, but her, never. If anything, I still loved her, was still in love with her, even more than before. And as husband and wife finally kissed, tears rained down my face silently, along with everyone else gathered to celebrate this joyous occasion.

Me and My Appetite

I was sitting with Angie at Dunkin' Donuts taking my time, as neither one of us was in a big hurry to get to work. Angie was having black coffee and an old-fashioned but I was going for broke: a hot chocolate with whipped cream and two mocha-frosteds. Gotta do something to spice up your day when all you have to look forward to is eight hours of sitting in front of a computer terminal with no one saying anything to you except, "Don't your eyes kill you, looking at that screen all day?" or "I don't know how you do it with those nails of yours."

Angie and I don't talk much in the morning. It's bad enough to have to be up and dressed before noon; at least Angie understands it would be too much to expect me to be civil about it. We just meet at some dive before work to fortify ourselves and give each other the once over. You need a girlfriend to tell you if your seams are straight, if your earrings match, if your slip is showing.

We finished our donuts and whipped out our compacts and lipsticks in one smooth motion, like a dance. Angie tends toward orange, which you can only get away with if you have beautiful bronze skin like she does. I go more for pinks and reds. We flipped open our compacts with our left hands and swiveled our lipsticks up with our right. As I was outlining my upper lip, I saw Angie's eyes leave her mirror for a split second to glance over my head and then return to her reflection.

She finished doing her mouth, and scraping at a smudge on her chin with her index finger said, "Don't turn around, but we are being admired."

"By who?" I asked, moving my compact a little, like a rearview mirror that needed adjusting.

"By whom." Angie corrected me before rolling her lips inward and pressing them together to even out her lipstick. "By that young man at the counter." She pointed with her eyes.

I lifted my mirror for a better view. Crew cut, leather jacket, white T-shirt. "Christ, he looks all of sixteen," I muttered, patting a dab of powder on my nose. Angie put her works away and swiveled in her seat. "You ready?" she asked, lifting her jacket off the back of her chair.

"Yeah, yeah." I was still fiddling with my face when our not-so-secret admirer turned on his stool to reach for a napkin and there in his profile was just the faintest outline of breasts. I gave a little gasp. Our *he* was a *she*.

"Girl, what is so fascinating about your face this morning?" Angie was on her feet, one high heel tapping with impatience. "Are you coming or what?"

"Or what," I said, catching the little butch's eye in my tiny mirror. Her face was openly curious and I gave her a little wink that said, *hold your horses, baby, I'm coming.*

"Angie," I put my compact down. "Will you please tell Mr. Franklin I have car trouble and I'll be a little late?"

"What?" Angie looked at me and then over my head at the counter for a minute. Angie knows boys don't interest me in the least, so she must have seen what I saw because she sighed and shook her head. "That's the third time this month, Sally," she said, giving me one of her tsk-tsk-tsks. "What do you want to go playing with her for, when you got a good woman waiting for you at home? And besides, Sal, she's jailbait."

"I'll make sure she's of age," I said, like Angie was my mother. "And anyway, Angie, variety is the spice of life and I can't help it if I have a hearty appetite." Angie has never understood this. Hell, a woman who always has a plain donut and black coffee for breakfast can't possibly understand the pleasures of jelly-filled, coconut-dipped, chocolate-frosted or vanilla creams. Luckily Angie doesn't have to understand. The only one who has to understand is Bonnie, and she understands just fine. Bonnie is a dream come true. She doesn't mind sharing me as long as I follow the rules: not in our house, not in our car, no staying out all night and no follow up phone calls or love letters. And most important of all, Bonnie doesn't want to hear about it. Angie thinks we're nuts and she's always throwing me that Paul Newman crap—why go out for hamburger when you've got steak at home—but hey, it's worked for me and Bonnie for thirteen years, so who is Angie to knock it?

"So, what is it this time?" Angie picked her pocketbook up off the table. "Flat tire, muffler problems, fan belt, carburetor..." She counted off the possibilities on her long orange nails that glowed under the florescent lights.

"Umm...let me think." I tried to remember what I had told Mr. Franklin last time. I really should write this stuff down.

"She's waiting," Angie said, tapping her foot again. "She just got a refill."

"Oh, just tell him I'm waiting for Triple A to come give me a jump start. Everyone knows that can take all day."

"You won't have to wait all day to get jumped, believe me." Angie fluffed out her hair and gave me a little wave. "Don't do anything I wouldn't do."

"Oh c'mon, Angie, I want to have some fun."

Fuck you Angie mouthed. Then she blew me a kiss and was gone.

I lifted my compact and opened it again to check out my affair-du-jour. I caught her reflection in my mirror and ran my tongue lightly over my lips. Her eyes widened. Then I snapped my compact shut and rose as if I was leaving. I lifted my coat from the back of my chair and folded it over my arms, but instead of walking toward the door I merely lowered my butt onto Angie's still-warm seat, so that now, despite the fact that we were across the entire restaurant from each other, my girl and I were face to face.

"More coffee, Miss?" A waitress appeared with a fresh pot.

"No thanks. I will have another donut though."

"What kind?"

I didn't hesitate. "Vanilla cream.."

My baby butch was watching me for a sign but I wasn't ready to give it to her yet. The waitress brought my donut over and it looked luscious: two light brown golden cakes joined together with sugary white cream swirled inside and overflowing the top in a tantalizing peak. Even though I'd already had two donuts, this was a challenge worth rising to the occasion for. And like I've already told you, I do not eat like a bird.

Without taking my eye off the girl in the wings, I darted my tongue out and licked the white cream once, and then once again. Through the din of coffee being poured, cash registers ringing and newspapers rattling, I could swear I heard that butch moan. I dabbed my middle finger into the cream and then put it into my mouth up to my first knuckle, sucking gently and rocking my finger in and out of my mouth ever so slightly. My girl slid off her stool a little and then regained her balance, propping herself up with her elbows on the counter and resting her helpless head in her hands.

I looked at my donut, licked my lips, and then, locking eyes with my baby butch, I brought that donut up to my mouth and proceeded to lick and suck the creamy filling out of that pastry with as much passion as I've ever felt in my entire life. My little dyke leaned forward wild-eyed, half rose out of her seat and practically did a somersault headfirst over the counter.

When I was done, I patted my mouth delicately with a napkin and without bothering to reapply my lipstick, I opened my purse for a cigarette, which I placed between my lips. At last my poor baby knew she was welcome. She bounded across that greasy floor in two seconds flat, flicking her Bic.

"Sit down," I said, accepting her light and gesturing to the empty seat across from me. We looked at each other for a minute. Her eyes were burning. "You look mighty hungry," I said, delighting in her blush. "What's your name, lover?" I asked, putting my hand on top of both of hers. She was hanging on to Angie's empty pink packet of Sweet 'n' Low for dear life.

"Sonny," she breathed, interlacing her fingers with mine.

"Sonny," I repeated, kicking off one shoe. "With an O or a U?"

"Oh," she moaned, as my bare foot rode up her leg underneath her jeans. I took off my other shoe and caressed her firm calves with my feet, silently thanking the Goddess that I had worn slingbacks that morning. Some of my shoes have so many buckles, even Houdini would have a hard time getting out of them.

Sonny's calves felt firm, like she worked on her feet all day. "You want some of my donut, Sonny," I said, for it was a statement, not a question. The poor girl could only nod. "C'mon, then." I put my shoes back on and rose. Sonny was at my side in a second. Someone sure raised her right. She helped me on with my coat, standing behind me while I took my hair out of my collar and gently teased her face with it.

"Where we going?" Sonny asked, eager as a puppy, as we left Dunkin's.

"You got a car?" I asked.

"Yeah," she said, half turning, "but it's a few blocks back that way."

"Never mind," I said. I didn't need her car; I needed to know she was over eighteen, though to tell you the truth, I don't know if I could have turned back at this point. "You're old enough to drive?" I asked, putting my hand on her arm. "How do you keep looking so young and handsome like that? Your skin is soft as a baby's." I traced her blush with my index finger.

"I don't know," she mumbled. "Just lucky, I guess."

"Oh, you're lucky," I agreed, taking her arm again. "Real lucky. In fact," I purred, stroking her arm through the sleeve of her leather jacket, "you have no idea how lucky you are."

I steered her toward a door, which of course she pulled open for me. "The Easton Mall?" Sonny was puzzled.

"Do you care?" I asked, looking around. "I mean, are you in a hurry?"

"No," Sonny said, and I stopped walking to thrust my hands onto my hips, pretending to be insulted.

"I mean yes," she stammered, mortified at offending me. I shook my head and rolled my eyes, as if I was disgusted that all she ever thought about was sex.

"Yes and no." Sonny was helpless, which is just the way I wanted her.

"Good." I started walking again. "I didn't think you'd mind if I picked up a few things."

I steered her through the light crowd of young mothers pushing strollers, junior high kids cutting school and bored housewives looking at dishtowels, until we came to Macy's. We passed housewares, juniors (where I paused briefly to admire a teal suede skirt) and sleepwear until we came to lingerie.

"Now, let's see." My hands swam through the racks, gliding over satins and silks. "What do you think of this?" I held a black longsleeved, button-down nightshirt, cut like a man's pajama top up to my chest.

"Oh no," Sonny said. "That's all wrong for you."

"Really?" I pulled my hand away from my body to study the outfit at arm's length. "You pick something out, then," I said, pretending to be disappointed as I hung the monstrosity back on the rack.

"How about this?" Sonny lifted a hanger full of red lace and feathers and held it toward me. "I've got a charge card here," Sonny boasted. "I'll buy it for you."

"Silly girl." Butches don't know the first thing about shopping. "I have to try it on first."

"Oh." She looked disappointed but her face lit up when I said, "Find a size fourteen and I'll meet you in the dressing room."

I took off my coat and waited for Sonny. I didn't have to wait long.

"Here," she said, proud as anything. I took the negligee and pushed her gently, my hand against her chest. "Now you wait out there until I have it on and then you can tell me what you think."

I closed the curtain between us and called, "Now don't go 'way," as I let my skirt drop to the floor in a puddle at my feet. Sonny could only see me from the knees down, but I was sure her eyes were glued to the ground as I let blouse, bra, slip, stockings and panties pile up in a heap. I stepped back into my heels and slipped the teddy over my head. It fit perfectly: the lace cups lifted and squeezed my breasts to maximum cleavage and the sheer material fell over my torso in silky folds, ending in a hem of feathers dusting the tops of my thighs.

"Come in," I sang from behind the curtain.

Sonny stepped inside and slumped against the wall, her watery knees buckling.

"Do you like it?" I breathed, twirling around so the teddy flared out, giving Sonny a peepshow of my glorious bush and derriere.

"You look beautiful." Her voice cracked. "Shall we wrap it?"

"I'm not sure." I turned away from her to consult the mirror. Sonny stood behind me, her reflection drooling. "I'm not sure about this strap," I said, shrugging my shoulder a little, which caused the strap to slide down my arm. "Can you adjust it for me?"

Sonny stepped forward and her trembling fingers touched my flesh at last. I caught her hand and moved it from my shoulder to my breast. She caught her breath in a loud gasp and I had to shake my finger at her. "Shh," I whispered. "We don't want a flock of salesgirls in here asking us if we need any help, do we?"

"No ma'am," Sonny whispered, starting to shrug off her leather jacket.

"Leave it on," I caught her to me in a full body hug and gently nudged her head down to the nape of my neck. She nibbled her way down to my nipple, spent some time there and nibbled her way back up again in search for a kiss on the mouth but I save these two lips for Bonnie so I just lifted the naughty nightie up over Sonny's head and from then on, there were no complaints. Sonny licked and sucked my entire body until that cream-filled donut had nothing on me, let me tell you. I was just about to explode when we heard footsteps which stopped right outside our dressing room. The voice that belonged to those sensible shoes asked, "Are you finding everything you need?" to which Sonny replied, "Oh yes," and proceeded to find them all over again.

Finally Sonny came up for air with a sticky grin. "Yum yum, " she said, wiping her mouth on her sleeve. "Finest breakfast I ever had."

I laughed. "I like a woman with a big appetite," I said, watching the lust stream from her eyes.

"What are we having for lunch?" Sonny asked, imagining I'm sure, spending the rest of the day, if not her life with me.

"Well, let's see," I pretended to ponder. "Why don't you see if this outfit comes in powder blue?"

"But red's definitely your color," Sonny said, a little whine creeping into her voice.

"Variety's the spice of life, sugar." I opened the curtain and shooed her out. "Light blue, baby. To match your eyes."

"Okay." Sonny took off and I got dressed fast. I had already made sure that the teddy only came in red and black, so I had a little time, because if I knew Sonny, she would rather die than come back to the dressing room empty-handed.

I straightened myself out and peeked out from behind the curtain. I could see Sonny with her back to me shaking her head as some poor saleswoman held up a light blue, full-length slip which was close, but no cigar. Grabbing my chance and my purse, I slipped out of the fitting room, out of the store and out of the mall, and ran down the street toward the office, which is no small feat in three inch heels.

I was only an hour and twenty minutes late for work, which wasn't too bad, considering. I passed Angie at her desk and hissed, "Meet me in the bathroom."

"Do I smell?" I asked when she came in.

"Pee-yew!" Angie wrinkled up her nose. "So tell."

I told, with Angie shaking her head and interjecting "unh-huhs" in all the right places. "So you left the poor girl all alone in a lingerie department with a salesgirl trying to make her quota?"

"Yeah." I filled a paper cup with water and took a long sip. "You know how heartless I am."

"So that's it for Dunkin Donuts." Angie folded her arms. "You know Sonny'll be there watching for you every morning for at least a month."

"I know." I tried to do something with my hair but my reflection said *freshly fucked* no matter how I combed it.

"And we can't go to Denny's anymore or the International House of Pancakes either." Angie shook her head. "Sally, what am I going to do with you?"

"Feed me toast and coffee in the car," I said and Angie laughed. "That would be the only way to keep you out of trouble."

"Did Franklin say anything?" I touched up my lipstick.

"Nah, but we better get back to our desks." Angie looked at her watch. "Only an hour until lunch."

"Thank God. I'm starving."

"You and your appetite." Angie led the way out. "You want to grab some chow mein at that place on Fifth Street.?"

"I can't," I said as we walked toward our station. "Remember the redhead?"

"Oh God, here we go." We stopped at Angie's desk. "What about the pizza place on the corner?"

"No good."

"The Deli on Third?"

"Unh-unh."

"The Taco Villa on Forest?"

I shook my head.

"Sally!"

"What can I say?" I shrugged helplessly. "Me and my appetite."

"We better go to my house for leftovers," Angie said.

"Sounds good. What'cha got?"

"Sally, what do Bernice and I always eat on Wednesday nights?"

I didn't even have to think. "Spaghetti."

"So that's what we got."

"I'll take it." I'll never understand Angie and Bernice. Seven years together and they eat the same thing every week: pot roast on Mondays, chicken on Tuesdays, spaghetti on Wednesdays... Don't they ever want anything different? There's no accounting for taste I guess. And anyway, who am I to judge? And besides which, Angie makes the best spaghetti sauce this side of the Mississippi. I'd do anything for a serving of it. Even leave Angie's girlfriend, the beautiful buxom butch Bernice in the capable hands of the chef.

The Flirt

Rose Weinstein was flirting with non-monogamy. Actually, she was flirting with the tall hipless wonder over by the pool table, whose crewcut she would love to run her bare feet through some lazy Sunday morning with the sun streaming in the bedroom window through the venetian blinds. But Rose was a married woman, a happily married woman. She'd been faithful to her wife for eleven years and had no intentions of straying now. But Terri was out of town on business at the moment, leaving Rose a bachelorette for the weekend. And there was no harm in flirting. Or was there?

Flirting dyke style of course meant that whenever the baby butch in the corner looked in her direction, Rose would lower her eyes, only to look up a minute later to catch the woman staring at Rose for the briefest of seconds before it was her turn to look away.

Rose crossed her legs, making sure her black skirt stayed at a respectable height along her thigh. She swiveled her bar stool around, took a sip of her beer, and swiveled back toward the pool table again. As if on cue, the woman across the bar picked up her pool stick, dipped it toward Rose, and sunk the eight ball right into the side pocket. Rose smiled in spite of herself. Smooth, very smooth, she thought, as she watched the pool shark hang her cue stick on the rack on the wall and bum a cigarette from one of her friends. Rose turned back around and finished her beer, pretending to remain calm as the woman slid her perfect, jean-clad ass onto the empty stool next to her.

"Hi, I'm Bobbi." Bobbi looked Rose up and down with the chutz-pah only a twenty year old dyke possesses, lust and admiration streaming from her eyes. Why, the woman was practically drooling. "I knew I'd never forgive myself if I didn't meet you tonight." Bobbi ground her cigarette out in a disposable silver ashtray and leaned her elbows on the bar.

To err is human, to forgive is divine, Rose thought, staring at the ashtray and feeling Bobbi's eyes undressing her. Would Terri forgive her? Or more importantly, would Rose forgive herself?

"Penny for your thoughts," Bobbi said, still looking at Rose with dark bedroom eyes.

Rose turned toward Bobbi. "Oh, they're worth much more than a penny."

"How about another beer then?" And before Rose could stop her, Bobbi called the bartender over and ordered a beer for Rose and one for herself. "What's your name?"

"Rose."

"Ah, a rose by any other name would smell as sweet." Bobbi picked up her beer and clinked it against Rose's. "Shakespeare. *Romeo and Juliet.*" She winked and Rose felt the pit of her stomach drop. "Here's looking at you, kid."

"Bogart. *Casablanca.*" Rose took a long sip of beer, conscious all the while of Bobbi's eyes on her throat, as she tilted her head back with the bottle against her lips.

"You're very pretty," Bobbi said, looking right into Rose's eyes as she put her beer down. "Would you give me the pleasure of taking you out to dinner next Saturday night?"

"You're very sweet," Rose was tempted to pat Bobbi's hand in a motherly fashion. "And I'm very married."

"Drag. Are you monogamous?"

"Quite."

"Bummer. Monogamy equals monotony," Bobbi said. Rose noticed she was also wearing a *silence=death* T-shirt. "So, if you're married, where's your wife?"

"Terri's out of town for the weekend. On business."

"Oh yeah?" Bobbi's eyebrows shot up and she leaned closer to Rose. "Well, what's good for the gander is good for the goose, know what I mean?"

"Not really," Rose lied.

"I mean, while the cat's away the mouse will play." Bobbi took her hand away from her beer bottle and started stroking Rose's fingers. Bobbi's hand felt cold and warm at the same time. "I really dig older women."

"Even one old enough to be your mother?" All of a sudden Rose felt like Mrs. Robinson.

"No way!" Bobbi laughed. "How old are you, thirty-two, thirty-three?"

Rose laughed too, flattered, even though the lesbian thought-police in her head were scolding her for being so politically incorrect. "I'm forty-three," she said, adding silently, *old enough to know better*, as she slid her hand away from Bobbi's. Bobbi's hand continued stroking the air where Rose's fingers had been for a split second before grasping her beer bottle again. She sighed dreamily, took another sip and grinned at Rose. Rose shook her head slightly. She had to admit, it did feel good to be so openly...so openly...desired. A slow blush crept over Rose's cheeks and down her neck. She knew this was no hot flash. Bobbi continued to stare at her, licking her tongue around her lips for an instant, as if to lick a drop of beer from her mouth, or as if to...

Rose looked away, trying to compose herself. When was the last time Terri had looked at her like that? Not that she had any major complaints about their sex life, but...well, after eleven years, things were slightly predictable. And God only knew what tricks this hot young thing had up her sleeve. Young, dumb and full of cum, that's what Terri would say. Rose looked up at Bobbi once more, who was still smiling away. Would I really risk my eleven year marriage for a rush of hormones, she asked herself, as a warm, pleasant feeling took over her belly. No, of course not. Eleven years. The feeling inside Rose's belly was spreading dangerously. But oh, those hormones. She squeezed her thighs together tightly. Listen, you can't have everything, Rose reminded herself, sounding like her own mother.

"So how come your wife lets you out by yourself on a Saturday night?" Bobbi asked, running a finger down Rose's sleeve. "Isn't she afraid someone will snatch you up and sweep you off your feet?"

"I'm not by myself. I'm with my friends, Loretta and Cammy." Rose gestured toward the dance floor. "They're just occupied at the moment."

Bobbi turned in her seat to watch a few dozen couples dancing groin to groin as Patsy Cline crooned a slow song through the speakers. "Wouldn't you like to be so occupied?" she asked softly, tilting her head to one side. "I'm very attracted to you."

Rose felt her belly burning. "Listen," she forced herself to say. "You're awfully cute. Why don't you go find someone your own age to play with? I'm sure there's at least twenty-five women in this very room that would give anything to dance with you."

"Aw, you don't take me seriously. I'm not a teenager, you know." Bobbi stuck her lower lip out and Rose's heart threatened to melt. Please don't do that, she silently pleaded. I love when butches pout.

"No, you don't take me seriously," Rose said. "I'm married." She held up her hand. "Ring and all."

"Wow, that's so patriarchial." Bobbi took Rose's hand again, to study her ring this time, so Rose let her. "Did you really promise never to have sex with anyone else ever again for the rest of your life?"

"Well, that's not quite how we put it," Rose said, trying in vain to ignore the little shivers that contact with Bobbi's flesh was sending down her spine. A vision of her and Terri's commitment ceremony, like a movie preview flashed across Rose's mind. There she was, standing next to Terri under the chuppah, her mother sobbing on one side of them, and Terri's parents stone faced on the other.

"But how can you be sure?" Bobbi asked, tracing the circle of gold around Rose's finger. "I mean, what if someone better comes along?"

"Life is full of missed opportunities," Rose said, thinking, *and you, my dear are one of them.* Now she *was* patting Bobbi's hand.

"But," Bobbi leaned in and lowered her voice to an intimate whisper that was barely audible above the music, the clacking of pool balls, and the fifty or so conversations going on around them. "Don't you ever get bored? I mean, how can one woman satisfy you for all those years? Don't you, like, miss the excitement of a first kiss?" Bobbi's face was in fact practically close enough for a good juicy smack on the lips. Rose very deliberately once more pulled her hand away. Of course sex was somewhat routine after eleven years, but that was a small price to pay for the love she and Terri had for each other, for the life they had built together. "A kiss is just a kiss," Rose said with a smile, picking up her beer bottle and clinking it against Bobbi's. *"Casablanca* again."

"My point exactly." Bobbi also took a swig of beer. "What's the big deal about kissing someone else? I just don't get monogamy." Bobbi shook her head. Obviously the challenge was on. Now she was going to try the philosophical approach. "I mean, you go out for coffee with other women, right? You have long intimate conversations with other women. You get massages from other women. You probably even go to the hot tubs with other women. So why not take the friendship one step further? I mean what's the big deal? JoAnn Loulan says an orgasm is just a muscle spasm."

"You're very well read," Rose said. *"Lesbian Sex,* and Shakespeare. I'm impressed." Rose traced the neck of her beer bottle with her fingertip and said, almost to herself, "That's it. I'll just tell Terri I had a muscle spasm with another woman. No big deal."

Bobbi's face lit up for a second until she realized that Rose was only kidding. "C'mon. Dance with me."

"All right." Rose slid off the bar stool. There was nothing wrong with dancing to a fast song, was there? Madonna's voice oozed through the speakers, urging Rose to express herself.

Bobbi took Rose's hand and led her onto the dance floor. They squeezed into the crowd of dancers and started moving their bodies, not making contact with more than their auras, but still feeling the heat between them. Rose wished she could freeze the scene, like an old *Twilight Zone* episode, walk off with Bobbi, fuck her brains out and then come back to the bar and resume the action, no one the wiser, no harm done. But unfortunately, this was life, not an old TV rerun.

The music changed to a slow song and Bobbi opened her arms. Rose walked toward her, shook her head and continued walking, back to the bar with Bobbi at her heels. Rose perched on her bar stool and Bobbi stood right in front of her, close enough for Rose to feel Bobbi's breath on her cheek. "Last call," Bobbi whispered. "We could really make some beautiful music together."

Rose placed her hands on Bobbi's shoulders and leaned forward. Bobbi shut her eyes, all ready for the kiss that Rose placed delicately on her cheek instead of her lips. Bobbi opened her eyes.

"Sorry," Rose said, indeed feeling more than a little sorry. "Maybe in my next life."

Bobbi stared into Rose's eyes for a long moment, and then finally admitted defeat. She took Rose's hand, raised it to her lips and kissed it. "Tell Terri I said she's a lucky woman."

"I will."

"See you." Bobbi dropped Rose's hand, gave a little wave and walked off, with Rose's eyes glued to her gorgeous tuchus. Too bad, she thought, youth is wasted on the young. Rose let out a deep sigh, remembering her father saying the very same thing at least a hundred years ago. She looked at the clock on the wall, hanging next to a sign that said, "No One Is Ugly After 2:00 am." It was eleven-thirty. If she left now, she could be home before midnight and give Terri a call. Suddenly Rose missed Terri very much. Her heart was glad she'd made the right choice, even though her loins weren't at the moment. Oh well. That would pass. Rose wondered if she should tell Terri that she, like Jimmy Carter, had lusted in her heart after another woman. "Well, for God's sake, I'm married, I'm not dead," Rose said out loud to no one in particular. The world was full of beautiful, sexy women, and tomorrow night her arms would be full of one of them. The one she had chosen. The one who had chosen her. The one whose dark eyes and full lips and large hands and small breasts were as familiar to her as her own tiny curved reflection in the half-empty beer bottle in front of her. Familiarity breeds contempt, Bobbi would probably say, but Rose disagreed. Absence makes the heart grow fonder was more like it. And with that thought in mind, Rose slipped off her bar stool to find Loretta and Cammy and tell them it was time, high time to go home.

Music To My Ears

When I stepped out of the shower and heard Anita Baker's voice crooning "You Bring Me Joy" I knew I was in big trouble. Melissa always puts *Rhapsody* on the stereo and cranks up the volume when she's in the mood. She had undoubtedly lit candles in our bedroom and sprawled herself between the sheets stark naked, or worse yet, all decked out in that ancient black negligee I'd bought her for our first anniversary a million years ago. I know Melissa's overtures should bring *me* joy; I know I should feel happy to be so obviously wanted, so needed, so *desired.* I know I should feel like tearing out of the bathroom and racing through the apartment dripping wet, only to dive head first onto our queen size orthopedic mattress and take Melissa in my arms. But if the truth be known, what I really felt like doing was stepping back into the bathtub and turning the Amazing Shower Head we'd just bought at Sears on full blast for about an hour, or until we ran out of hot water, or until Anita Baker shut the hell up, whatever come first. Then Melissa would get my message as clearly as I was getting hers.

I took my time toweling myself off, combing out all two inches of my hair and shaving my arm pits. I wasn't in a big hurry to face Melissa and her not-based-in-reality ideas of how our sex life should be. After all these years she still didn't accept the fact that passion waxes and wanes and that I no longer want her every two seconds like I did the first year we were together. I knew as soon as I stepped into our bedroom we'd have one of our famous sex fights and believe me, that was not something to look forward to. I delayed the inevitable by bleaching my mustache and trimming my nose hairs and then, as there was absolutely nothing left to do in the bathroom except perhaps re-tile the floor, I shrugged on my terrycloth robe and opened the door. Time to face the music, which by the way was still the melodious voice of Ms. Baker, who had moved onto a song entitled "Been So Long." Thanks a lot, Anita.

I crossed the apartment and cautiously let myself into our bedroom. As I suspected, there were enough lit candles on top of our bureaus to set off the fire alarm, a stick of cinnamon incense was sending a sickeningly sweet swirl of smoke into the air, and a big lump which I could only assume was Melissa, lay motionless under the covers in the middle of the bed. Well, here goes nothing, I thought, rooting through the top drawer of my dresser in search of a clean pair of underwear. "Want me to drive into town for bagels and the paper?"

"No," said the lump.

"Want me to make some coffee?" I asked, fishing a pair of sweat socks out of my second drawer.

"No."

It looked like monosyllabic answers was the theme of the morning. Okay, fine. I'm no fool. I knew what Melissa wanted. But I didn't want the same thing. At least not right now. Was that so terrible? All I really wanted was to be sitting outside on our porch with my feet up, the *New York Times Book Review* in one hand and a poppy seed bagel smeared with cream cheese in the other, the sun warming my face and a cup of hazelnut decaf steaming at my side. What was wrong with that? Plenty. I knew I should have kept my big mouth shut.

"You should want *me* for breakfast," Melissa shrieked, throwing the covers aside and leaping out of bed in all her glory. "What is wrong with you?"

"Nothing is wrong with me," I stated flatly. I thought I'd try the calm, rational approach this morning. Another mistake.

"Then there must be something wrong with me." Melissa stomped over to the full-length mirror hanging on the back of our bedroom door and started inspecting herself. "Of course you don't want me. Who would?" she asked in a disgusted voice. "Look at me.

My breasts are all saggy, my stomach is all flabby..."

"Melissa, would you please? There's nothing wrong with you. Now c'mon, stop."

"I don't know..." While she contemplated herself in the mirror, I pondered my next move. I had on my underwear and a pair of socks, and it was time to remove my robe. If I took my robe off and didn't get my T-shirt on fast enough, Melissa was sure to interpret that as a change of heart. On the other hand, if I pulled my jeans on up under my robe before removing it, Melissa would know I had already made up my mind. To dress or not to dress, that was the question. Though it was clear to me that it really didn't matter. No matter what I did, Melissa and I were going to fight this morning and it was bound to be a doozy. Well, when in doubt, I reasoned, do nothing. So, still fully robed, I sit down heavily on the edge of the bed. "Melissa," I said gently, "there's nothing wrong with either of us."

"Then why do we have this problem?" she asked her reflection in the mirror, who was momentarily distracted by a pimple on her chin.

"We don't have a problem. I'm just not in the mood."

"You're never in the mood. How can you say that Lesbian Bed Death isn't a problem?"

I swear on my nonviolent soul, that somebody should shoot JoAnn Loulan or whoever it was that came up with that term. "We do not have Lesbian Bed Death," I hissed through clenched teeth, despite my valiant effort to remain in control. "We've had sex twice this month."

"When? I don't remember." Now Melissa was putting a French braid in her hair.

I stood up and got my datebook which was on top of my bureau, next to a pocket comb and a spill of loose change. Lately I'd been putting exclamation marks on the days we'd done it, to use as ammunition for times like these.

"Let's see." I scanned several weeks-at-a-glance. "We had sex after we went to the mall three weekends ago..." (There was nothing like finding a good bargain to get Melissa all worked up) "...and the weekend before that, after we went to see that art exhibit, 'Therapists

Express Themselves.'"

"I don't remember." Melissa, finally bored with herself, plopped down next to me on the bed. "Let me see." She grabbed my calendar, glanced at it and then threw it across the room. "Oh, what's the use? Obviously if I have to look at the goddamn calendar, it wasn't worth remembering."

"Melissa, you never remember. How can it be so important to you if you don't even remember when we do it?"

"I don't remember," she spat out the word *remember* like someone who had accidentally eaten a whole tablespoon of unsweetened Baker's chocolate. "I don't remember," she repeated, "because it's always so boring." She fell back on the bed. "Me on my back, you on your back, I come, you come, did we miss *Saturday Night Live?*"

Now she was getting nasty. I love *Saturday Night Live.* "Melissa, what do you want from me? Leather and lace? Whips and chains?"

"No." She folded her arms and turned on her side, offering me her back. "I just want a little excitement, a little tease, a little sexual *tension* for a change, that's all." She let out this great big sigh, like her life was almost over. "You know, like Samantha."

"Samantha is an idiot." Melissa was all curled up, so I addressed the backs of her knees. "Every dyke in town knows she's not working overtime three nights a week. Every dyke but her girlfriend that is."

"Yeah, I know it's wrong. But still..." I could practically hear the dreamy look in Melissa's eye. "At least she feels desired. At least she knows somebody *wants* her."

"I want you, Melissa. You know that."

"No, I don't know that. You never show it. Not like Cynthia wants Samantha." Another deep sigh. "The woman is so damn happy all the time. It's like sex is oozing out of her every pore. You can practically smell it on her. Christ, the other day two dogs followed her home."

"If that's what you want, just pick up a pound of raw hamburger," I mumbled under my breath.

Melissa sat up. "What?"

"Nothing," I said. "Aren't you cold?"

"No, I am not cold. Jan, are you listening to me?"

"Yeah, yeah, yeah. The erotic as power and all that." I almost said all that *crap* but that would definitely have sent Melissa through the roof. Lately she'd been leaving all this reading material on my pillow: *The Erotic as Power, Bushfire, Lesbian Passion* and the latest issue of *On Our Backs*. I read it all, and it's not that I don't think Audre Lourde was brilliant, mind you, or that JoAnn Loulan doesn't have some interesting things to say. It's just that their work loses a little something when it's thrown in your face as indisputable proof that there's something wrong with you because you're not fucking your girlfriend enough.

Melissa was looking at me, waiting. "Can't we just give it a rest, Melissa?" I hated the pleading tone that had crept into my voice. "C'mon, it's a beautiful Sunday morning, let's not ruin it by fighting. Let's go out. C'mon, I'll treat you to brunch."

"Yeah, we can give it a rest all right." Melissa pried herself off the bed. "We can give it a rest for the rest of our fucking, or should I say non-fucking lives."

I knew where this was leading. "Are you going to be nasty to me all day?"

"Well, that depends." Melissa pulled on her underwear and a pair of shorts. "Are you going to go to couple's counseling with me?"

No fight would be complete without bringing up therapy. "Melissa, if we had an extra eighty-five bucks to throw out the window every week, I'd rather re-do the floors..." my voice rose, "...or fix my back tooth, or get a new couch..."

"You're going to need a new couch," Melissa screamed twice as loud as me, "because I'm taking the old one with me."

"And just where do you think you're going?"

"I'm leaving," she yelled at the top of her lungs. "I'm not living out the rest of my life as a sex-starved lesbian. God, what is the *point* of being a dyke if you never even get to do it?" She screeched the word IT for a good thirteen seconds until it reverberated off the bedroom walls and practically punctured my ear drums.

Shit. I pulled on a pair of jeans, threw off my robe and dragged a T-shirt over my head, while Melissa banged open her bureau drawers and finished getting dressed. "Melissa, please calm down. You're not going anywhere. Now come on."

She looked straight at me and said very softly, "Then I'm having an affair."

I stopped, halfway to the closet, my robe dangling off one finger by its hook, and looked at her. Not that Melissa hasn't threatened cheating before, mind you. It wasn't what she said, but the way she said it, that stopped me in my tracks. Usually Melissa shrieked the word "affair" in the same glass-shattering pitch she had screeched the word "it" a moment ago. Then she would burst into tears and whisper that she really didn't mean it, that the only person she really wanted to have an affair with was me. And then I'd hold her and stroke her and comfort her with all kinds of promises I had every intention of keeping, but somehow never could. It wasn't all my fault though. I read enough of Melissa's damn psychology books to know that we were polarized on the issue, with her always wanting it and me never wanting it, neither stance being completely true. But somehow, when it came down to it, it was always my fault.

Suddenly our bedroom got awfully quiet. Even Anita Baker had finally shut up. Breaking away from my usual anal-retentive tendencies, I let my bathrobe unhook itself from the edge of my finger and silently slide to the floor. "You're serious," I said to Melissa, my words a statement, not a question.

"I don't have a choice," she said in the voice of a woman whose mind was already made up.

"Fine. Go." I flung open the closet door. "And take this with you. And this. And this." I started flinging things over my shoulder: our vibrator, Melissa's black lace naughty nightie, a pair of edible underwear that were supposed to be cherry flavored but tasted like cough syrup. "I wouldn't want you to have a lousy time," I said, my voice an ugly sneer. "Oh, and don't forget this." I stomped into the living room, snatched that damn Anita Baker album off the stereo and split it over my knee. "If I never hear this goddamn record again, it'll be too soon," I yelled, flinging the pieces behind me as I marched through the living room, the dining room and the kitchen, all the way out the back door.

There. I had done my part. I'd acted like an enraged significant other was supposed to. But if the truth be known, I pondered as I sat at a small outdoor café with the paper and some decaf, I felt completely ambivalent about Melissa having an affair. On the one hand, maybe she'd get off my back (not that she'd spent much time on it lately). In fact, I'd even heard from some expert that sometimes having an affair could actually save a marriage, for reasons I have yet to understand. Of course this expert was a guest on the *Oprah Winfrey Show* and had probably gotten his degree by sending in a coupon from the back of a comic book, but still...

On the other hand, the thought of my Melissa in the arms of some other girl was almost more than I could bear. But the key word here, ladies and gentlemen, is almost.

Two hours later I dragged my heavy heart home. As soon as I opened the door, I heard the steady creaking rhythm of the living room rocking chair.

"Here." I held out the *New York Times Magazine Section,* a peace offering. "I saved the crossword puzzle for you."

"Put it on the table." Melissa gestured with her head. "I was serious, Jan," she said, continuing our discussion as though I had never left the house.

"I know you were. You're going to have an affair."

"Don't you care?" She looked up at me and I couldn't tell if her eyes wanted me to say yes or no.

"I don't have a choice," I said, with no anger in my voice. "But remember, no double standards."

"What do you mean?"

"I mean, if you can have an affair, I can, too."

"What?" Melissa stopped rocking. "But you don't even like sex."

"Says who?"

"Well, you never want to have it."

"That's not true. Anyway," I flopped down on the couch, "let's not start again, okay? We now have an open marriage."

"Fine." Melissa grabbed a section of the newspaper and disappeared behind it.

The following Friday night, after a less than delicious dinner of macaroni and cheese, Melissa vanished into our bedroom while I did the dishes. Just as I was sponging off the stove, she emerged dressed to kill as the saying goes, but dressed to fuck was much more like it. She was wearing her tight black leather jeans with a short black velvet jacket, and when she moved I could see a red lace something or other splashed across her chest. It looked to me like Melissa wasn't wearing a bra, and suddenly it dawned on me that she probably wasn't wearing any underwear either.

"Going out for groceries?" I asked her back as she passed me on the way to the bathroom.

"In a manner of speaking." I followed Melissa into the bathroom and stood in the doorway with my arms folded, watching her outline her eyelids in purple, until she turned from the mirror, asked "Do you mind?" in a huffy voice, and firmly shut the door.

"Do I mind?" I muttered, stomping into the living room. "Of course I mind." I threw myself onto the couch, turned on the TV and ignored the blurry images dancing in front of my misty eyes. Here was my girl, my very own Melissa, looking hotter than all the dykes in the latest issue of *On Our Backs* put together, going out without me, and I wasn't supposed to mind? Shit.

Finally I heard the bathroom door open, the click of Melissa's fuck-me heels across the kitchen linoleum and the jangle of her keys as she took them off the hook by the back door. Wasn't she even going to say good-bye to me?

"I'm going," she announced from the living room doorway.

"What am I supposed to say: Don't forget your dental dams? Have a good time?"

"Sarcasm doesn't become you," she said, fluffing out her hair. I almost snapped back, "Infidelity doesn't become *you*," but I would have been lying. Melissa looked absolutely gorgeous and she already glowed like someone who'd been up all night with a new lover doing the nasty in thirty-seven-thousand ways. Maybe it was the anticipation, hopefully it was just make-up.

"Don't I get a kiss good-bye?" I asked like a pathetic five year old who doesn't want her mother to go out and leave her with some stupid babysitter. Melissa moved toward me, almost drowning me in her perfume, and kissed the air around my cheek. Now, Melissa usually air-kisses me when she's wearing lipstick and usually I don't mind. But usually she wears lipstick when she's going to work or going out with some other femmes on a shopping spree. Usually she isn't going out to find herself a new lover.

"Jan, I know this isn't easy for you," Melissa stepped back from me, her voice more gentle than it had been all week. "I want you to know..."

"Just go," I hissed through clenched teeth. If she was going to go, I wanted her gone long before I started bawling my head off, and that gave her about two-and-a-half seconds. As soon as I heard the door shut, I started howling and I didn't let up for the better part of two back-to-back reruns of *Roseanne*.

Finally I got sick of hearing myself moaning and groaning, so I dragged myself off the couch. It was only a little past ten, according to the bagel-shaped ceramic kitchen clock my mother had bought me and Melissa for our last anniversary. I tried to comfort myself with a few spoonfuls of mocha-chip ice cream eaten straight out of the carton, but the ice cream was as tasty as mud. And without Melissa around to yell, "Jan, will you please use a dish?" it just wasn't any fun at all. I went back to the living room and tried to distract myself with *20/20*, but to tell you the truth, I really didn't give a damn about whatever Barbara Walters was going on and on about.

Maybe I should call someone, I mused, but who else was sitting home all alone on a Friday night? And more importantly, who on the entire planet did I trust enough to tell this sad story to? I wasn't exactly bursting at the seams to admit to anyone that Melissa was out there looking for a good fuck because she wasn't getting enough at home. Besides, before I could make a call, I'd have to find the phone which was easier said than done. Ever since we got a cordless phone, which Melissa thought was the greatest invention since platform shoes, I spent half my life looking for the damn thing. Now I, being a creature of habit, always return the receiver to its cradle. But Melissa, also known as the original Chatty Cathy Doll, will leave the phone anywhere; in our closet on her shelf of fuzzy sweaters, in the kitchen on top of the toaster oven, even in the bathroom on the back of the toilet. Whenever the phone rings, Melissa yells, "Go!" and we both start racing around the apartment in hot pursuit. I think at one point, Melissa was even keeping score.

Oh Melissa, Melissa, Melissa. The whole house screamed her name: her clogs kicked off in the middle of the living room floor where I was sure to trip over them; a half-filled glass of cranberry juice, its rim lined with her lipstick sitting on the kitchen table. Any way you looked at it, I was crazy about the woman. I couldn't help it if I was no longer a lean, mean sex machine (was I ever?) like the hot young stud that was probably leading Melissa around the dance floor this very minute. I was sure Melissa had gone to Amelia's, as there wasn't another dyke bar around for a good fifty miles. I could just see Melissa being swept past the jukebox by some smug stallion, her strong arms holding Melissa tight, her lips zooming in to caress Melissa's flesh...

Suddenly it was all too much for me to bear. I couldn't just sit home while some young slut who didn't know any better was ruining my life. I ran out of the house without even running a comb through my hair, jumped into my car and tore up the highway. Good thing there were no cops on the road. I could imagine one pulling me over. "Where's the fire, young lady?" he'd ask in a burly voice, and I'd have to tell him the truth: "The fire, officer, is in my heart."

I pulled into the parking lot and immediately spotted Melissa's maroon Chevy Spectrum snuggled up next to a blue Toyota pick-up. I almost parked on the other side of her, but then decided against it. What if someone walked her out to her car and started making it with her under the moonlight? I better not take any chances, I thought, pulling into a spot under a lone tree far from the maddening crowd.

I got out and slowly sauntered my way through the parking lot. I may have made great time on the road, but I lost a good twenty minutes standing at the door, my whole body a quivering mass of hesitation. Did I really want to go inside and risk seeing what I most dreaded I would see? As I stood there trying to muster up my courage, I heard two women come up behind me, and with them my moment of truth had arrived. I either had to step aside and let them pass, or go in ahead of them. The point was, either way I had to move, even though my Reeboks felt like they were filled with wet cement.

I pulled open the door...and stepped back. "Evening, ladies," I said, waving them inside. They looked so young, so happy and so excited to be going out together on this fine Friday night, I almost puked on their puppy love. *Just wait until you've been together for seven-and-a-half years,* I wanted to yell after them. But instead, I tucked my tail between my legs and slunk inside behind them, shrouded in the safety of their two-headed shadow.

As I waited to give my three dollar cover charge to the baby-faced bouncer at the door, I craned my neck, but luckily it was too dark to see anyone. Or to be seen *by* anyone, come to think of it, as I suddenly realized I hadn't even splashed cold water on my tear-streaked face, let alone ironed my shirt. No matter, though. I wasn't here to impress anyone, I was here on a mission: Operation Bring Melissa Home.

After the bouncer waved me in, I headed over to the bar and ordered a beer. Hell, I might as well try to enjoy myself for two minutes before I got down to business. Melissa and I hadn't been out to Amelia's in a long time. Every once in a while, one of us would say over dinner, "Let's go out tonight," and the other one would say, "Sure, fine." I mean, it always sounded like a good idea at seven o'clock, but by the time ten-thirty rolled around, one if not both of us would be in our pajamas. We'd make jokes about being old married farts and that would be the end of it.

I took a swig of my Bud and scanned the crowd, squinting my eyes through the blue haze of cigarette smoke. There sure were a lot of good-looking women out tonight. Hey, maybe I wouldn't even look for Melissa. If she could have her fun, then I could have mine. Maybe I'd just pick somebody up myself. I studied the crowd again, playing "what if" with myself. What if I was single? What if I had just a tiny bit more chutzpah than the cowardly lion in *The Wizard Of Oz?* Who would I really go for? My eyes flirted from face to face and then land-ed on a dazzling dyke standing in the corner. She was leaning against the wall with all her weight on one long leg, her arms were folded across her more-than-ample chest, and every once in a while she tossed her short blonde hair in a way that was supposed to look casual but was more than likely rehearsed. Hmmm. I ran my fingers through my hair in what I hoped was a sexy gesture, though what I was really doing was making sure I didn't have any Alfalfa-like cowlicks sticking out in a million different directions, like I had just dragged myself out of bed. Though come to think of it, maybe that's not such a bad idea, I thought, letting my hand drop. Let her think I spent half the night horizontal. She doesn't have to know I spent the last few hours prone on the couch sobbing, not smooching. I drained my beer and swallowed a belch behind my hand. Did I have the nerve? Just as I was about to make my move, a slick-haired butch in a leather jacket took my love-interest's arm and led her away. My eyes followed them onto the dance floor as they started to slow dance next to a couple who were both wearing black pants and sleeveless red tops. How cute, I thought. Another totally enmeshed lesbian couple emulating the Bobbsey Twins. Then I woke up like someone had just poured a whole pitcher of ice cold beer over my head. Melissa had left the house in red and black. My Melissa. Where the hell was her jacket? And who the hell was she dancing with?

I leapt off the bar stool, crashed through dozens of cuddling couples, and crossed the entire dance floor in two seconds flat. Just as I reached them, Melissa's dance partner lowered her head, her lips all puckered up for a kiss. And to my utmost horror, my very own darling girlfriend did not turn away.

"Hey!" I grabbed Melissa by the shoulders and spun her around. "Melissa, what the hell do you think you're doing?"

Her dark eyes widened. "Jan, what are you doing here?"

"Taking you home." I grabbed her elbow and steered her through the crowd, leaving the woman she'd been dancing with in the dust.

"Wait, my jacket." Melissa tried to pull her arm away.

"The hell with your jacket." I pulled open the bar door and dragged Melissa through the parking lot over to my car. "Get in," I ordered, unlocking the door.

"No."

"I said get in the car."

Melissa must have seen that I meant it, because without a word, she yanked open the passenger side, got in and slammed the door behind her.

I slid in behind the wheel, but my hands were shaking too badly to start the engine. After two tries I just threw my keys on the seat between us. "I can't believe you were in there kissing someone, Melissa. How could you do that to me?"

"You said I could, remember? I believe your exact words were, 'Now we have an open marriage.'"

"I don't care what I said," my voice exploded. "I didn't think you'd really do it."

"Well, what did you think?"

"I don't know. I didn't think."

"Well you shouldn't have come to the bar." She folded her bare arms stiffly.

"What did you expect me to do while you were out on the town? Sit home and watch TV?"

"Sure, why not? That's what you do every night."

"Don't start with me, Melissa, and don't change the subject. We're talking about you, damn it." I pounded the steering wheel for emphasis. "You were in there half naked for God sakes, kissing another woman!"

"Were you jealous?" she asked lazily, like a fat cat quite pleased with herself.

"Of course I was jealous!" I placed both my hands on her two shoulders and shook them. "How could you?"

"Will you relax?" Melissa put her two hands on top of mine. "It was hardly even a kiss."

"Hardly my ass."

"Oh, c'mon. It was just a teeny, tiny kiss. An eensy, weensy peck on the cheek. It wasn't even a smooch."

"Are you sure?"

"Yes, I'm sure. Look, I'll show you." She leaned forward and kissed my aura. "Like that."

"Bullshit. That's not what I saw."

"What did you see?"

"This." I grabbed a fistful of hair at the back of Melissa's neck, leaned her head back, locked lips with hers and kissed my girl for all I was worth. At first she didn't respond, but when I didn't let up, she threw her arms around my neck, opened her mouth and pressed her soft body into mine with that special little moan of hers I hadn't heard in ages. And that's all it took to start me fumbling with her buttons and snaps and zippers and for her to do likewise with mine, and before you could even say the word "affair" we were going at it in the front seat like two teenagers with raging hormones who had to get the car home by eleven or else they'd be grounded for a month. For one second, the thought that Melissa was fantasizing about the woman in the bar flashed through my mind like a comet, but to tell you the truth, I didn't care. All I cared about was holding her close and pressing my lips against the side of her neck, with my fingers sunk deep inside her. And then when she pushed me back to climb on top, I didn't even give a fuck that the car keys were digging a ditch into my back and the stick shift was gouging my thigh. All I cared about was the sweet fact of Melissa and me being together.

After we both came about forty-seven times, Melissa sat up and beamed at me. "You do want me," she said, immensely pleased with herself.

I leaned up on my elbows. "Of course I want you."

"No, I mean you *really* want me." She traced my lips with her finger. "Pretty clever of you, parking all the way back here."

"Yeah, it was, wasn't it?" Hell, I'd never tell.

Melissa pulled me up into a sitting position. "Think you can repeat that performance sometime?"

"I'll sure as hell try."

"What do you mean, try? Couldn't you just say, 'Sure, anytime,' or something?"

"Melissa, don't start with me, okay?" I should have known one good fuck wouldn't solve all our problems. "Can't you be happy right now?"

"Oh, okay." She lifted my hand and kissed it. "Want to take me home?"

"I don't know." I squeezed her hand. "Are you sure you're ready to come home?"

"I'm sure." She turned from me to face front and buckle up like a good girl, while I felt under my ass for the keys. "Wait a minute. I left something in the bar."

I tensed. "Some*thing* or some*one*?"

"My jacket, silly. And what about my car?"

"We can come get your car tomorrow." I didn't want Melissa out of my sight for a second.

"Yeah, but I love that jacket. Besides, it set me back fifty bucks." Melissa started buttoning, snapping and zipping herself up. "Come in with me."

"Like this?" I could only imagine what I looked like.

"Sure, c'mon." She got out of the car and I sure as hell wasn't going to let her go back in the bar alone. I followed her through the parking lot, tucking my shirt into my pants. When we reached the door, Melissa pulled it open and started to laugh. "Listen."

"What?"

"They're playing our song."

"What song?"

"'Same Ole Love.' You know, it's on my Anita Baker album. It's a sign," Melissa said, happily pulling me by the hand onto the dance floor. I took her in my arms and whispered into her hair, "I'm sorry I broke your record, baby," as our bodies swayed together. "I'll buy you another one."

"You better," she looked up at me, "because I'm going to be playing it a lot more often from now on. Okay?"

"Okay. It'll be music to my ears," I said, and to prove it, I worked my leg between Melissa's thighs and kissed her long and hard, not letting her come up for air until the song was over.

The D.J.'s Girl

It was a dive, but it was our dive. It would have been a hole in the wall, but it wasn't big enough. It was darker inside than outside, especially when a half or even a quarter moon hung low in the sky. But hell, at least it was some place to go besides your own living room which was also small and dark except for the blue light of the television flickering halfway across the room and the orange glow of the cigarette butt smoldering in the bottom of the empty beer bottle beside you. At least you knew you'd find company in the bar. If not somebody to hold, at least somebody to talk to. Or somebody to look at, anyway.

It didn't even have a name, the bar. Either you knew about it or you didn't. Like I said, it was dark. Looked like anybody's place sitting on the side of the road. But inside, oh inside, you knew it was someplace special. As soon as you paid your two bucks and walked through that doorway, it was like St. Peter had opened up the pearly gates and let you step inside your own personal heaven.

Inside the bar, women who had meekly said, "Yes sir," all week to some sloppy, cigar-smoking senior VP who couldn't type his own letters if his life depended on it, now held pool sticks in their hands with all the confidence of a dozen James Deans. Here, women who walked down the street with their heads down, mumbling, "Excuse me," and avoiding eye contact at all cost, stood with their hips cocked, arms crossed and beer in hand, surveying the scene with cool eyes like they owned the goddamn joint. Here, women could let their hair down without being afraid some guy would run his smelly fingers through it. Here in the bar, after a forty hour plus work week, women could relax among their own.

So that's how it was every Friday night and every Saturday night for as long as I can remember, and I go way back, let me tell you. I was here back in the days when no one said the word queer unless they were looking to take it outside, put up their dukes and have one good fight. I'm still hardly used to the word dyke, let alone queer, never mind an entire group called Queer Nation, whatever the hell that means. I was here before Stonewall and I'll be here long after the gay nineties are over, if I'm lucky enough to live that long. Hell, I'll be here as long as I got two legs to stand on and if I don't, I'll just make some-one drive over to my place, pick me up and prop me against the wall of the bar. Unless the bar closes of course, which is something I don't even wanna think about. But Flo, the owner, has been having a hard time lately. Business ain't so good.

"I gotta do something, Nan," she said to me one night as she sloshed her rag back and forth on the bar in front of my elbows. "Gotta get more of the young ones in here. You old timers just can't put 'em away anymore and my cash register shows it."

"Why don't you charge another buck or two at the door?" I asked, already deciding to give up my once a week fancy lunch at Friendly's so I'd be able to afford my two nights out.

But Flo shook her head. "I already get complaints about having a cover at all. You know how it is. I can't be charging what it costs to go to a goddamn movie or something. No, I got a better idea."

"What?"

"I'm thinking of getting a D.J."

"Really, a D.J.?" I automatically swiveled in my stool to stare at the juke box halfway across the room. The juke box was older than I was and had all our favorite songs on it; Elvis, the Everly Brothers, Patsy Cline. I didn't want no D.J. coming in here playing heavy metal or Madonna or who knows what else. But Flo's mind was already made up and the D.J. was starting the following weekend.

So it was with some fear and with more than a little trepidation that I made my way to the bar that Friday night. Flo had put flyers up all over town and as soon as I stepped out of my car, two women with matching crew cuts, nose rings and combat boots asked me, "Is this the club?" Now to me, a club is something that I've been hit over the head with back in the good old days which weren't all that good, believe me. But to these youngsters who looked like they should be drinking milk and cookies, not beer and pretzels, a club was some place to go.

"This is it," I said, letting them step ahead of me before I went inside. There sure were a lot of women in the bar. The shoes I had on my feet were older than most of 'em, but other than that the bar looked pretty much the same. Flo had set up a big empty table in the corner for the D.J. who was due to arrive any minute. And the pool tables were pushed a little closer together so there'd be more room to dance. I'd heard that Flo wanted to take one of the pool tables out altogether, but some of the over-fifty gals had threatened to lay right down on top of it rather than let it be hauled away. I mean, a person can only take so much, right? Anyway, Flo gave in and the pool table stayed.

I made my way over to the bar, ordered my usual beer and leaned back against the counter to check out the scene. No sooner had I taken my first swig of brew then the back door of the bar opened and a woman carrying a big box in both hands stepped inside. She looked around like she was lost for a minute, but then she spotted the empty table in the corner and made her way over to it. The D.J. I watched her pass about a dozen times back and forth, in and out, hauling all kinds of shit inside: turntables, tape decks, CD players, amps, mixers and then boxes and boxes of music. I was exhausted just watching the woman and she was no twenty-something, let me tell you. She looked as old as yours truly, but that didn't stop her. She just kept going back and forth, doing her job like a little ant, ignoring all the heads that swiveled this way and that, quietly watching her. Then she went out the back door one last time and didn't come back. I wondered if something was wrong. Everyone went back to their drinks or their girls, but I kept my eye on that back door, waiting. After about ten minutes had gone by, I decided to go out there. Who knows, maybe the D.J. was in trouble. The bar isn't in the best neighborhood in town, and it wouldn't be the first time some young punks with too much alcohol and testosterone in their blood picked a fight on a Friday night.

But that wasn't it. The D.J. was perfectly intact. She stood beside her car with these two big black boxes that came up to her waist in front of her. The speakers. They were made of wood and they looked solid, like they weighed about eighty pounds a piece. How she'd gotten them out of the car and onto the ground was something I didn't even want to think about. She just stood there looking at them, and probably hoping they'd grow legs and walk on into the bar themselves. There was no way she, or any other girl, or any guy for that matter, could do it.

After a minute I cleared my throat and asked, "Need some help?"

The D.J. turned to look at me and the way her face changed made me almost say out loud, "How do you spell R-E-L-I-E-F?" like the commercial, but I didn't want to hurt her pride. She was a proud woman, I could tell, and she certainly didn't wanna be asking for help on her first night out. Hell of a way to make an impression. So, it killed her to say, "Yeah, thanks," but it was either that or risk spending the rest of her life in traction. Those suckers were heavy, let me tell you. Thank God they had handles, one on each side. The D.J. grabbed the right handle and I grabbed the left, and by the time we got that hundred pound piece of sound inside the bar and across the floor, my arm felt like it had been pulled right out of its socket. After I helped her with the first one, I almost told the D.J. she'd have to find someone else to help her with the second one, but I steeled myself and just did the deed. After all, it's been said in some circles, that I'm a proud woman, too.

I sat at the bar, wiped my forehead with the back of my hand, ordered another beer and watched the D.J. set up. Besides being part moving man, she was part electrician, too. I've never seen so many wires. This one went into that speaker, that one came out of this amp. She slung patch cords and extension cords around and over and under and through, until just watching her made me dizzy. But she just kept on. She was a diligent woman, and a handsome one, too. Short, slicked back hair, fresh pressed pants, crisp shirt, shiny shoes. The kind of woman that makes the butches in the room sit a little closer to their femmes and put their arms around them, just like the femmes are always asking them to. But more than a few girls in skirts slipped off their stools and out from under their butch's arm, saying, "Be right back, baby," as they made their way across the floor. They said they were going to check out the music, but checking out the music maker was much more like it.

But the D.J. paid them no mind. Even the femme with the highest heels and the shortest skirt who leaned over one of the speakers and asked, "Got dinner plans later on?" was answered with, "I'm not sure. Who sings it?" leaving her with egg all over her face as she walked away in a huff. No, the D.J. was all business, playing what everybody asked for, young and old alike. She was being tested, let me tell you, but she passed with flying colors. She had everything in those boxes, from rock 'n' roll to rap. She even had "Green Door," which nobody can ever find at the radio station when I call up to request it during oldies hour on Thursday nights. I even got out there to shake my booty when she put that one on, and I haven't asked a woman to dance since saddle shoes went out of style. Hell, everyone was having a great time, even my old pal, Trudy who danced so hard she threw her back out in the first hour, and had to sit in a corner the rest of the night, holding an ice pack one of the young jocks got out of her car against her hip. Trudy just turned her grimace into a smile as more than one young thing fawned all over her, asking if she was all right and did she want another beer.

Around midnight the crowd started thinning out. Flo's right, us old gals can't stay up til the wee hours of the morning like we used to. The young ones can still party until dawn though, and the D.J. adjusted her music, as the kids who still looked like they needed babysitters filled the dance floor flailing about, their arms and legs flying. Not my idea of dancing, but to each their own, as they say. Most everyone I know had already gone home, but I'd made up my mind to stay and see if the D.J. needed help hauling all that shit back out to her car. How she got it out of her car and into her house after spending the whole night on her feet was beyond me. But hey, that wasn't my problem.

So I ordered my last beer about twelve-thirty or so, and then about ten minutes after that, something happened to the D.J. You couldn't tell, unless you'd been watching her all night like I had, but she started acting different, like she was on the alert for something. Or someone. Her ears were cocked and even though she didn't turn her head, her eyes kept going to the door. Even the hairs on her head stood up just a little bit straighter. At exactly quarter to one, she put Patsy Cline's "Crazy" on the turntable, stepped back, and held her breath.

As if on cue, the door to the bar swung open, and this doll of a woman walked in, in heels, hair and a little black dress. She didn't bother giving her two bucks to the bouncer, but flung the words, "I'm with the D.J." over her shoulder as she swung her hips right on by. She was a good looking woman, with big brown eyes, and full red lips, a little bit of a thing, five-foot-two maybe, including the three inch heels. The kind of woman that makes the femmes stand a little closer to their butches and hook their hands through the crook of their arms and hold on, the way we're always asking them to. But there was no need to worry. The D.J.'s girl walked right across the dance floor holding out her hand and the D.J. came out from behind all that equipment to lead her around the dance floor as graceful as could be, like two skaters gliding across the ice. It was like a show, watching them. And then when the song was over, the D.J.'s girl went and stood right behind the turntables, shaking her little body in time to the last few songs the D.J. played, until it was one o'clock and time for all of us to call it a night.

So then the D.J.'s girl perched herself on a little stool and whipped out a nail file to keep herself from getting bored as the D.J. broke down. Wires and cords were unplugged, and tapes, CD's and records were put back in their boxes. Then I watched the D.J. do everything in reverse. Back and forth, in and out with the amps, mixers, CD players, tape decks and turn tables. And then when it was all done except for those mother speakers, I jumped down off my bar stool, hitched up my sleeves, and strode over, all ready to give the D.J. a hand. But before I could even get a word out, the D.J.'s girl picked up a two ton speaker, slung it on her hip like it was nothing but a bag of groceries and trotted out to the car with it, heels and all. My mouth dropped open in amazement, and before I could shut it, she was back for the other one, slinging that speaker over her shoulder like it was a god-damn pocketbook. The D.J. held the door open for her as polite as can be, with a proud little smile playing across her lips. But her smile was nothing compared to Flo's, who stood behind the door grinning like her face was about to fall off. Flo knew she had it made. Word spreads fast as peanut butter in this town. Soon everyone and her sister would be flocking to the bar to shake their ass to the D.J.'s music. And not only that, they'd be sure to stay all night long, just to get a glimpse of the D.J.'s girl.

What I Will Not Tell You

If you want to hear all the luscious, gory details, forget it. You know I don't talk about those things. I'm just not that kind of girl.

So don't even ask me how I happened to walk into the bar at eleven-thirty last Saturday night dressed in a sleeveless red mini-dress looking like I was out to get something. Or someone. I'm not going to tell you. I'm not one to spill the beans.

I'm not even going to tell you how I spotted her way over at the very end of the bar, or how somehow I could see her plain as day through the dim lights and all that lazy, hazy cigarette smoke that was drifting between us. You can ask all you want, but I have no intention of telling you how I knew she was the one even before the bartender set down a drink in front of me and nodded in her direction.

I will tell you, since you must know, that I did go over and say thank you, and she did answer you're very welcome, but I will not tell you any more about our conversation. And I most certainly will not describe her yellow shirt and how it set off her tan, or her tight jeans that hugged her gorgeous thighs, or her black cowgirl boots complete with spurs, because I am sure if I did I'd never hear the end of it.

Since you are so incredibly nosy, I will tell you that yes, we did dance, but even if you beg, I will not divulge what happened when a slow song came on. I will not describe how soft her lips felt as she pressed them hard against mine because they have not yet invented words to describe such a thing. And likewise, since I am not a poet, I couldn't even if I wanted to which I don't, tell you what her arms felt like tight across my back and how her thigh felt sliding itself between my legs and how her breasts felt pressing up against mine underneath her thin cotton shirt.

Even if you begged and pleaded on one knee I couldn't tell you who else was in the bar that night, because frankly I didn't notice. I can and will tell you that there was no one in the bathroom when I went in to powder my nose, but I won't tell you who knocked on the door a minute after I went in there.

You'll have to guess who came in and stood me gently but firmly against the wall, covering my body with hers and kissing me on the mouth like there was no tomorrow. You'll have to guess who ran her hands up and down my body and whispered oh baby and snuck one of my breasts out the top of my dress and sucked on it like it was a lollipop and she was a kid who never had anything sweet before in her entire life. You'll have to guess who pushed my legs apart and was thankful that I was wearing stockings and a garter belt underneath that little red dress but nothing else. You'll have to guess whose hand reached up and in and whose three fingers I held onto like my life depended on it. You'll have to guess who called me baby doll and told me to give it to her and who thrust her hand in and out faster and harder until I had to bite her neck to keep from screaming. And you can try to figure out just who it was that wiped my cum down the side of her jeans and watched me in the mirror with a big grin on her face while I pulled my dress down and combed my hair and put on a fresh coat of lipstick which she promptly kissed right off.

Since I suppose you must get your kicks somewhere, I will tell you that we left the bathroom and went back to the bar and had another drink, but I would never in a million years tell you that I sat on her lap and let her play with me in the dark under my little red dress looking prim and proper the whole time while the bartender mopped up a few spills with her soggy towel and chatted to us about this and that. And even if you promised me the moon, which I know you won't, I'm going to plead the fifth amendment and keep quiet about what happened when another slow song came on and we moved into a corner and locked our thighs and lips together, not caring if everyone and her mother knew what we were doing. No, I will not tell you that we stayed in that dark corner long after the song ended and that her hand snuck itself inside my dress to find my stiff nipples and her knee snuck itself between my legs and took me to a place I'd never been before.

But since you are so very curious, I will tell you that when the bar closed she did walk me out and hail a cab and slip the driver ten dollars to take me home. And she most certainly did open the car door for me and give me a very respectable goodnight kiss.

So don't ask me any more questions, especially what her name was, because even if you had a fit on the floor I would not tell you even if I knew it which I don't, though I very well might find out when I return to a certain bar at a certain time next Saturday night. Let's just change the subject right now because I am not a kiss and tell type of gal, never was and never will be. If you want to hear that kind of talk, you'll just have to go ask somebody else.

PART IV: MS. DYKE AMERICA

With Anthony Gone

I didn't mean to do it. It wasn't premeditated or anything and it wasn't exactly a crime. It was just incredibly politically incorrect and totally weird besides. I'm not sure what it means if anything, except this: death sure does some really strange things to people, including me.

I didn't want to go to Anthony's memorial. Hell, does anyone ever really want to go to a funeral? First of all, he died at a really inconvenient time: I had used up all my sick leave and had to take an unpaid day off work. Second of all, I had to drive into Manhattan, which in my opinion is about as much fun as jumping off the Brooklyn Bridge and just as dangerous. And third of all, if I went, I would have to admit that Anthony was dead, something I'd been avoiding for two months, ever since Mark left that message on my answering machine: "I'm calling to tell you what you think I'm calling to tell you." Thanks a lot, Mark. You could have put it more gently: "Hi Joanne, Anthony passed away this morning." Or, "Hi Joanne, Anthony's no longer among the living." Or even, "Hi Jo, Anthony's gone." Oh hell, I guess it really doesn't matter how he said it, and even I know it's pretty lame to be mad at Mark for his choice of sentence structure. Anthony's dead and that really pisses me off. And what can I do about it? Nothing and that makes me even madder. If I ever stop being so goddamn angry, I'll probably be incredibly sad and that's just not my style, so I just kind of blocked out the whole thing, which is exactly my style. And besides, it's not very hard to do, since no one up here knew Anthony; he was part of my former life. A life that was very different than the one I'm currently living in several important ways. First of all, back then I was straight, which I know is hard to believe since I could easily win the Ms. Dyke America contest these days with my crew cut, nose ring and leather jacket and all. Second of all, back then AIDS was spelled with a Y and came in caramel cubes that were sold in drug stores and were supposed to make you lose weight. And third of all, Anthony was very much alive.

Anthony. When I met him, I was awed by him. He was easily the most beautiful person, male or female I had ever seen, with his huge dark Italian eyes framed with masses of lashes, his olive skin, his black shiny hair, snow white teeth, and that body that was built to last with mile high legs, a smooth torso, and biceps that rippled in the sun. Anthony was attractive all right, but I wasn't attracted to him. At that time, I had simply accepted the fact that I was a completely asexual creature. I knew men didn't do it for me and I didn't yet know that women were an option. So I was never in love with Anthony but I was definitely drawn in by his charm and I knew I wanted to be his friend.

We met in Boulder, Colorado one summer, two native New Yorkers totally out of place amid the cowboys and the mountains. Ironically, we met in a place called the New York Deli, which was anything but. I was waiting on line (out there they say "in line") when I heard a voice with that unmistakable accent declare, "An egg cream. No, it has nothing to do with eggs. Three squirts of chocolate syrup, two fingers of cream and top it with seltzer, all right lady? Don't bust my chops. And an order of fries. It's not for nothing I grew up on Staten Island." My heart leapt at the sound of someone from home. "Hey," I said, "I'm Joanne Bergman, from Brooklyn."

"Oy vey, a landesman," he said, proving you don't have to be Jewish to be Jewish as long as you grew up in New York. "Anthony Scarnici, from Staten Island. You want an egg cream, mamela? Make it two," he barked to the woman behind the counter. We sat and talked for hours, eating what I soon learned was Anthony's favorite meal: french fries dipped in a chocolate egg cream. Sounds terrible, I know, but believe me, it's good.

So as it turned out, Anthony and I were enrolled in the same poetry program, taught by none other than the great Allen Ginsberg. We got an apartment together and fixed it up as best as we could which wasn't very, since both of us were broke (this poetry program wasn't exactly cheap). After we both got beds and dressers for our bedrooms we had nothing left over for living room or kitchen furniture. Oh well. One day we found one of those huge old wooden spools from the telephone company on the street, rolled it home and voila! a kitchen table. No chairs though, so we mostly ate on the floor. Depending on who was cooking we'd either have matzo ball soup or spaghetti and meatballs, always the same argument accompanying the meal: were Italians dumb Jews or were Jews nerdy Italians? Obviously this was long before the days I worried about being politically correct or had even heard the term, come to think of it. Like I said, Anthony and I were thinking about poetry and furniture, which he combined in an ingenious manner: one day he came home with a styrofoam head he found on the street outside a wig shop and placed it on the mantle of our fake fireplace. Two days later, complete with a straw hat and wire-rimmed glasses, the head was a dead ringer for William Carlos Williams, the poet we happened to be studying. Our decor was complete when I brought home a child's little red wagon from the salvation army and poured a pan of water into it. For those of you who don't know much about poetry, I'll let you in on the joke: William Carlos Williams' most famous poem, which Allen Ginsberg (or Ginzy as we called him) drummed into our head all that summer was called "The Red Wheelbarrow." I can't quote it exactly since I never did pay that much attention in class, but it was something about how everything depended on this red wheelbarrow which was full of water, parked next to a bunch of chickens. The brilliance of this particular poem completely escaped me, but Anthony was quite taken with it, and recited it at least a dozen times a day. In fact, whenever anyone visited our little house for the first time, Anthony would run over to the little red wagon and begin flapping his bent arms up and down and squawking like a chicken, in order to see just how literary-minded our newest visitor was. No one but Ben ever passed the Red Wheelbarrow test, but Ben comes later on in the story.

So much for our literary careers. Anthony was quite talented actually; I wasn't. I only remember one poem I wrote that summer and now that I think about it, it's kind of spooky. One day I came home and Anthony was hysterical, which was nothing unusual. "Jo, my nerves are shot. Go in my room. Hurry."

"What is it, a spider?" I grabbed a shoe, being the butch of the family even back then when I didn't know the word. A minute later I came shrieking back to the living room. "Oh my God, Anthony, where did they come from?" The *they* I was referring to were hundreds, maybe even thousands of horse flies all swarming at Anthony's bedroom window, trying to get out.

"What do I know? Something must have hatched." He ran to the store and came back with two huge cans of RAID. "The hell with karma," he yelled and charged into his bedroom, spraying away. Now by this time, Anthony had become a quasi-Buddhist and believed in not killing any other sentient beings, lest God knows what would happen to him the next life around. So who got stuck holding the bag full of flies? None other than yours truly. At least I got one fairly decent poem out of it called *Flies:*

> Anthony and I discover hundreds
> of Woody Allen size flies
> clumped together like quivering blackheads
> on the white walls of his bedroom.
> "The hell with karma," he yells,
> running out to buy a can of Super Raid
> which we sprayed on the walls,
> windows, ceiling and carpet.
> "Raid kills bugs dead," I say,
> quoting the commercial and wondering
> what kind of brownie points we're scoring
> with whoever's in charge of our next life.
> Anthony refuses to meet my eye
> as I stand holding a brown bag full
> of half-dead sentient beings,
> their legs sticky and still kicking
> in the dying afternoon.

Not bad, huh? Maybe I could have been a poet. Anyway, isn't that weird? The only poem I remember writing that summer was about death and karma and all that stuff, and had Anthony in it to boot. I just think that's really bizarre.

Anyway, who knew what the future held that summer? We were young, we were good-looking...well at least one of us was. Anthony's attributes certainly didn't go unnoticed. He had a string of admirers, though none of them were as ardent as himself. It was not unusual for me to stumble out of bed in the morning and find him gazing at his reflection in the bathroom mirror wearing nothing but a shower cap, perched upon his head at a jaunty, beret-like angle. Anthony wouldn't leave the house until be looked absolutely perfect and he actually thought unattractiveness was a crime that should be punishable by law. "Will you look at that?" he'd grab my arm and point to some poor unfortunate, who not only wasn't blessed with good looks like Anthony, but was all decked out in lime green polyester besides. "Five years in the slammer, no parole," he'd bark over his shoulder, shaking his head as the walking fashion faux pas passed. I'm sure now that he's dead, people will talk about Anthony like he was a saint, but believe me, he wasn't. He never got on my case about how I presented myself to the world though, and believe me in those days I was not a pretty picture. I had long stringy hair that hung in my face (yes, I know it's hard to believe) and I wore the same thing every day: baggy jeans with a shapeless, faded T-shirt. I didn't really pay any attention to my appearance and neither did Anthony, which only further reinforced my suspicions: my body was of little consequence, just something that I was forced to lug around.

Anyway, if anyone should have been arrested that summer, it was Anthony, who roamed the streets in flimsy red silk running shorts or skin tight jeans with strategically placed holes. Either outfit left little to the imagination. It was always amusing to watch Anthony on the prowl. He'd see someone he liked, sidle up to him, stick his thumb in his mouth and pull it out real s-l-o-w-l-y. It worked every time and I spent many, many afternoons roaming the streets waiting for Anthony to give me the hi sign (a pink and black striped necktie hanging from our front door knob) so I knew it was safe to come home.

Everything changed when Mark entered the picture, though. When Anthony and Mark laid eyes on each other at the New York Deli, it was like time stood still. Anthony didn't even finish his egg cream before he made his move. And before I knew it, Mark had moved in with us (thank God he at least had some furniture). This was definitely serious: before Mark, Anthony never let any of his boy toys spend the night. He didn't want any of them to see him first thing in the morning before his face woke up and took its beautiful shape. Before Mark, I was the only one who got to see Anthony look human like the rest of us.

Mark and I became friends, too. After all we had a lot in common: we both loved Anthony. Still, I was beginning to feel like a third wheel, so luckily Ben came upon the scene at just about this time.

What can I say about Ben? He had eyes that could rival Liz Taylor's, dimples Shirley Temple would have died for, and extraordinary black hair that fell in ringlets past his waist. "My aunt Ethel always said it was a shame such hair was wasted on a boy," he told me, "so I grew my hair long to make her happy."

"And did it make her happy?"

"Don't ask," Ben said rolling his eyes, just like a member of my very own family, proving you don't have to be from New York to be a New Yorker, as long as you're Jewish. Ben became a regular at our house, especially on the nights when I cooked my famous matzo ball soup.

Ben entered the poetry program late—he was always late for everything—so he hung out with Anthony and me so we could catch him up on assignments. Anthony suspected he was hanging around with us for other reasons, too.

"He likes you," Anthony would whisper. "Go on, fuck him. I can't, Mark would kill me, so it's up to you. For God's sake, somebody has to do it."

"We're just friends," I'd whisper back, even though I wasn't really sure about that. Ben unnerved me. I knew he was attracted to me, and I was sort of attracted to him, but something held me back. Now, when I think about it, I know it was his gender (all right, call me sexist) but back then, all I knew was that he confused me. He was very feminine looking, and very gentle besides, which is what drew me to him. But whenever our bodies made contact, even casually, I immediately pulled away.

Once we were actually mistaken for a couple, in a funny way. The four of us were walking home from an open poetry reading, the kind that drags on and on and makes you swear you're never going to read, let alone write another poem in your life. Anthony and Mark were up ahead, as Anthony was constantly trying to give Ben and I the opportunity to be alone together, when out of nowhere a car pulled up, and heads yelled out the window, "Fags! Fucking dykes!" before roaring away. Anthony's response was to shriek, "We're homos! We're as healthy as the milk you drink!" and plant a nice, wet kiss on Mark's lips. Ben and I just looked at each other, speechless. Finally I broke the ice. "It must be your hair," I said, and just for the hell of it, took one of his ringlets and twirled it around my finger. I felt nothing, but later that night I did have a classic erotic dream of Ben and I twirled together in his hair, except of course Ben had breasts and all the other female trappings, becoming as my grandmother would say, the shayneh maidel of my dreams. But shortly after that night Ben cut his hair (at least his aunt Ethel would be pleased) and moved in with a poet named Christine, who I'm sure knew less than nothing about matzo ball soup.

At the end of that summer, Ben moved on to California, and Anthony moved back to New York with Mark in tow. I stayed put, due mostly to inertia, working odd jobs and trying to sort out my life. Finally I decided to move back to New York, where at least I could get a really good egg cream. Anthony was delighted. "It's not for nothing I work out at the gym five days a week," he said as we lugged cinder blocks up six flights of steps to build bookshelves in my new railroad apartment. Anthony thrived on city life, but alas, I didn't. The noise and the dirt and the crime got to me. "You need to meditate," Anthony had obviously kept up with his Buddhism. "You have to tame your mind." I actually allowed him to convince me to fork over a hundred bucks to attend a weekend meditation retreat on Lexington and twenty-third. There we sat on little cushions in a room full of other meshugenehs, listening to our teacher, whose name was Dharma or Karma, and who very much resembled a woman I had gone to high school with named Debbie Finkelstein. She gave a short shpeel on the Buddha, and then said we were to sit absolutely still with our backs straight for forty-five minutes, just following our breath. That was it? I looked at Anthony, thinking, *Here I am, in the most exciting city in the entire world, and I'm paying someone a hundred bucks so I can sit and do nothing?* I don't know if he read my mind, but all of a sudden, he smiled and then I smiled and then he started to laugh and then I started to laugh and we just couldn't stop. I'd get it together and settle down, and then he would, too, and a minute later I'd start to giggle again, and so would Anthony. Soon our laughter traveled around the entire meditation hall interrupting everyone's concentration and the teacher asked us to leave and that was that.

So, I left New York and moved up to a small New England town where there was not an egg cream to be found, even though at least half the population were transplanted New York Jews like myself who couldn't hack the city. And then one day I was sitting at Friendly's when the waitress took my order along with my heart, and I realized that lo and behold I was as bent as Anthony himself. Of course I wanted him to be the first to know. "It's not for nothing you hung out with me all those years," he said, which was a nice way of saying, I-told-you-so. "When do we get to meet the little woman?"

"Soon," I said, but soon never came. Lisa and I were completely wrapped up in each other (I finally realized that bodies did have some purpose after all) and by the time our relationship ended three years later I was a new woman. Not only was I a lesbian, but I was a feminist, and an angry one at that. I thought men were scum, straight, gay or otherwise. So gradually Anthony and I lost touch, except for the occasional birthday, Christmas or Chanukah card.

Years passed, how many I'm ashamed to say. I was in and out of several relationships, searching for Ms. Right and I'd become an English teacher at a very hip alternative high school where I could be out. I had long ago realized I really wasn't a poet, but teaching English suited me, and allowed me to indulge in my love of literature. One day, while thumbing through yet another obscure literary magazine that crossed my desk, I came upon a poem written by none other than Anthony Scarnici. Without a moment's hesitation, I picked up the phone and dialed Anthony's number which miraculously still lodged itself in the hard drive of my long term memory. Of course he wasn't there. Nor was he at the number the person who was there gave me. It took some doing, but finally I tracked him down.

"Hi Anthony, it's Jo from Brooklyn, remember me?"

"Of course I remember you," Anthony said in a strange voice. It was like he was talking in extra slow motion. I rolled my eyes. Was he sleeping at four o'clock in the afternoon? Or maybe on quaaludes (we had done our share of recreational drugs). Anyway, it was clear now was not a good time to talk. "I'll call you back and we'll make a date," I said. "I'd love to see you. How's Mark? How's your writing? Never mind, I'll call you tomorrow."

"Okay," Anthony said, adding something strange. "Mobility's a big problem right now, but you can come visit me. Just call first to make sure I'm up to having visitors. I have days and I have days."

And that's how I found out Anthony had AIDS. He'd been sick for over a year, so I guess he just assumed everyone he knew, knew. He found out unexpectantly, too. He went to give blood to get some extra cash and they ran a blood test and told him he was positive. Without any warning or anything, just like that.

Of course I went to see him right away. Mark opened the door and we fell into each other's arms and cried. Then I composed myself and walked into Anthony's bedroom. There he was, the boy whose theme song was "You're So Vain," looking like hell with yellowish skin, thinning hair and little red spots all over his unbelievably gaunt face. He motioned for me to sit on the bed. "I still do all my entertaining horizontally," he said with a wry smile. I had to move his legs to make room for me to sit down. He was so thin, and so weak, but still so Anthony. "Nice hat," he said, "let me see." I gave him my purple softball cap and not only did he try it on, but he admired himself in a hand mirror he kept by the bed.

I didn't stay long since he was obviously very tired. "Next time you come we'll go to the bookstore on St. Marks," he said and I said sure, even though I knew there wouldn't be a next time. A month after I saw Anthony he lost his eyesight and caught pneumonia. He went into the hospital and never came out. I meant to go see him but I just couldn't face it. I know it was selfish, but I just couldn't hack it. Dealing with difficult things, like my feelings for example, is not exactly my strong point.

So like I said, I didn't especially want to go to the funeral. But I had to. Because there was no one in my life I could talk to about Anthony. There was no one who would laugh when I said, "Remember the time Anthony got mad at Mark for taking a bite of his quiche and stormed out of the restaurant and made us search the entire city for him because he had the only house key?" If you didn't know Anthony, it just wouldn't strike you as funny. And I needed to be with people who knew Anthony. So I went. I kinda wanted someone to come with me, but I didn't know who to ask. I didn't have a girlfriend at the time, which is why what happened, happened.

The service was in a classroom of some community college, where Anthony had taught a poetry class years ago. There were lots of people there, but no one I knew. Friends of Anthony's, and a few relatives, like his sister who was a year older and looked exactly like him, and his mother and father, standing on either side of her. Mark finally arrived, but I couldn't get near him, as everyone wanted to pay their respects. Finally some music began and then Anthony's sister said a few words. Then one by one, various people stepped up to the front of the room. Someone sang a song, someone played a message Anthony had left on her answering machine, someone just hung onto the podium and cried.

And then I heard my name. "Joanne?" I turned around and there was Ben, who I hadn't seen since I left Colorado all those years ago. I had the same feeling I had over a decade ago when I saw Anthony standing in Boulder's New York Deli among all those strangers: a landesman. Somebody from home.

"Hi," I whispered, "late as usual." He grinned that dimpled grin and we grabbed each other in a big bear hug and cried. After a minute he squeezed me extra hard and then we let go of each other. Or almost let go. We sat there holding hands and it felt strange to be holding a man's hand. Strange and scary and wonderful. I felt a warm flush spread across my face and neck and down to various other parts of my body. I couldn't look at Ben. Stop it, I whispered to myself. Are you crazy? You're at a funeral. What kind of pervert are you? And besides that, you're a dyke.

I squeezed Ben's hand and he squeezed mine back. No doubt about it, he was thinking what I was thinking. My body was pulling a mutiny on me and there was nothing I could do about it. Without a word Ben and I rose and walked out, hand in hand. He led me to an empty classroom, and kicked the door shut. All thoughts stopped as he lifted me by the waist onto a desk and kissed me hard, for all he was worth. I dove into that kiss and before I knew what was happening, we were moaning and groaning and grabbing at each other's clothes as frantically as two teenagers in the back of a '57 chevy. Of course neither of us were carrying a condom so we didn't go all the way, but pretty damn close. Close enough to make us both come, which started us both sobbing in each other's arms again.

Eventually we composed ourselves and Ben shyly turned away from me to tuck in his various body parts while I did the same. We sat on the windowsill and Ben took a crushed pack of cigarettes out of his shirt pocket.

"I can't believe we just did that," he said, offering me a cigarette which I actually took, even though I don't smoke, but I figured what the hell.

"I know," I said. "I can just hear Anthony saying, 'I can't believe you guys finally did it at my fucking funeral.'" I shook my head.

"Yeah." Ben smiled and straightened my shirt. "Oh God, Joanne. What did we just do?"

I swung my legs back and forth. "I'll tell you what we didn't do," I said softly. "We didn't bring Anthony back."

"No," Ben sighed. "We didn't." He looked out the window for a while and then looked back at me. "So anyway," he tried to sound casual, "what have you been up to for the last decade?"

"Well, I've been a lesbian for seven years," I said, and that, combined with the look of shock on his face struck me as hysterically funny. I started to laugh and just couldn't stop and Ben cracked up, too. "Laughing and crying, it's the same release," I sang in an incredibly poor imitation of Joni Mitchell, which broke us up even more. What a day. Finally we calmed down, though Ben seemed kind of concerned about the whole thing, even more concerned than I was.

"Did I ruin it for you? I mean being a lesbian and everything, and me being a man and everything..." he fumbled for words.

"Well, the lesbian thought-police would kick me out of their club if they ever got wind of this," I said, "but what the hell. I don't know what came over me."

"Me either," Ben said. "I mean I have a wife and a kid and everything up in Vermont."

"Really?" For some reason now I didn't feel so bad. I guess it evened the score a little. Ben had something on me, but I had something on him, too. "So now what?" I asked. "We certainly can't go back in there." I pointed with my head.

"No," he said. "Want to go get something to eat?"

"I don't think so." I looked at him. "That would be too intimate."

He smiled. "Are you sure? I could really go for some french fries and a chocolate egg cream."

"Maybe some other time," I said, and pitched my cigarette stub out the window. "See ya," I said rising to go.

"See ya," Ben said, giving a little wave.

I turned and left the room and the building without looking back. With Anthony gone there was no one I really wanted to talk to. There was no one to share the great irony of the moment with and that was a real pity, let me tell you. With Anthony gone there was nothing to do but head up the street even though I had absolutely no idea where in the world I was going.

Still Life With Woman And Apple

You have been wandering around Gal's Gallery for barely an hour, yet museum fatigue has already set in. There is a stiffness about your neck and shoulders. Your feet are dragging as if through mud and your eyes are glazed over as though you have been up all night watching television. You park yourself on a hard bench in front of a painting: Still Life With Woman And Apple. You stare at the woman sitting on a maroon couch, one arm resting along the back of it, one leg crossed over the other, gazing at an apple on a small white dish on the table in front of her. Just for fun, you decide her name is Lilith.

From the way Lilith is looking at the apple before her, you know she is thinking about sex. Lilith thinks about sex all the time. Sex sex sex sex sex. Lilith thinks sex once a day keeps the doctor away. Lilith greets you on the street by pinching your ass and asking, "Getting any?" when a simple, "Hi, how are you?" would do. Lilith's philosophy is, straight people think we do it all the time, so why disappoint them? Lilith says if they're going to scream insults at us and throw rocks at us and take away our jobs, our houses, our children and our lives because of who we have sex with, we better make sure we're having a damn good time to make it all worthwhile.

There's a clock over Lilith's head. Both hands have stopped at the twelve. It is always midnight in Lilith's world, never noon. She is always dressed in black leather from head to toe: boots, pants and a jacket with lots of zippers, all of them unzipped.

You know this is Lilith's cruising outfit. You know she can sniff out a new dyke in town as easily as a kitten can find the catnip patch in a garden of weeds. You imagine her knocking at your door just as you finish unpacking your last carton of books, or right as you are placing the last cast iron frying pan on its hook in your new kitchen. She has left her Honda purring in your driveway, and invites you out for a ride. Reminds you to hold on tight as she takes you up the mountain to a secluded spot under a full moon and a sky speckled with stars. She teases you with a midnight picnic. "Want a hunk?" she'll ask, offering you a wedge of bread. "Take my cherry," she'll stay, extending a fistful of fruit. After the meal, she'll lie back on the grass, her hands under her head. "I'm so hot!" she'll exclaim, stripping off her boots, pants and jacket. All she'll have on underneath is a black leather G-string and a tiny rose tattooed on the left cheek of her ass.

Her body gleams in the moonlight. "Aren't you hot?" she'll inquire. You try not to let on that you are sweating profusely. Museums are always so stuffy. Stifling. No air. You can scarcely breathe. You loosen your collar. Unbutton your shirt. Shed your clothes as gracefully as a snake sliding out of her skin.

You approach the painting and place your foot on the bottom of the frame for a leg-up. You hoist yourself into the portrait and stare at Lilith. She has not moved She is still gazing at the apple in front of her. Her eyes reveal her hunger. She is starving. Ravenous. Famished. She has been staring at that apple for a very long time.

Just for fun, you decide your name is Eve. You lift the apple from its small white dish, and take the first bite. You chew voraciously until it is gone. Devoured. A part of you. You take another bite, and then another and then another until the apple disappears completely. The apple is now contained by you. The apple has now become a part of you. It is time for you to become the apple. You lie down on the table. Lilith has not moved. She is still still. She stares at you. At your red rosy cheeks, your breasts like two apples, the long stem of your neck, the apple blossoms of your hair. She is hungry. It is midnight. You have never been so still in your life. You know you are delicious. You wait for Lilith to take her first bite. You will gladly wait forever.

Around The World In Eighty Dykes

Life never turns out the way you expect it to, that's what I say. I know that's not an incredibly earth-shattering revelation, but hey, what do you want? I'm no big deal hot shot, professor of philosophy or anything. I'm just an ordinary pair of white cotton crew socks, and I'm not ashamed of it, either. There' s no sense in being all stuck up like a pair of No Nonsense panty hose. We all have to start somewhere, and I'm downright proud of my humble beginnings on the top shelf in the last aisle of Woolworth's in North Nowhere, Massachusetts. Everyone's gotta start somewhere, right?

There I was, minding my own business, just hanging around, when someone became quite smitten with me. That's how it happens you know, when you least expect it. "Ooh," I heard a soft voice croon, "a hundred percent cotton for one-dollar-forty-nine." The next thing you know I was swept off my feet, packed into a bag, and carried off.

That was all right, though. I loved Marsha. When I wasn't snuggled up with my sockmates in her third drawer, I was keeping her tootsies warm, which was no small feat, let me tell you: that girl's got circulation problems like you wouldn't believe. Also, she didn't get out much. Winters were hard in her neck of the woods, so after work Marsha was quite content to cozy up with a good book and a cup of hot chocolate. I was all settled in, enjoying the good life, when who should show up but Angel.

Now Angel was one of those young, breeze-into-town-breeze-out-of-town-that's-what-you-get-for-loving-me kind of dykes; I could just tell by the pack on her back and the sad state of her Birkenstocks.

149

They'd been around the block and then some, let me tell you. But my Marsha fell fast and fell hard and there was nothing to be done about it. That's the way it goes: the stay at home types go for the merry pranksters and vice versa. Keeps life interesting, I suppose.

So before I could protest, Angel was crashing at our place. That first night she spent exactly one hour on the fold-out couch in the living room before Marsha padded out of her bedroom in her pink bunny PJ's and whispered into the darkness, "Angel, are you awake? Listen, my bed's a lot more comfortable than that old sofa, and I don't mind sharing it. Really."

Well, Angel knocked Marsha's socks off in about two seconds flat. It was me and the bunnies on the floor from then on, let me tell you. For the next few months, anyway. Then spring arrived and Angel started getting restless. With summer came that look in her eye that said it was time to be moving on. It was festival season, after all, and Angel never missed Michigan. Marsha said she didn't mind, but I saw a tear leak out of her eye. Angel didn't notice of course. She was too busy packing.

"Here, take this," Marsha said, handing her a wool sweater. "The nights will be chilly out there. Take a pair of socks, too." And before I knew what was happening I was stuffed into Angel's backpack. What could I say? That's the way it goes. Just when you think everything's settled, life socks it to ya, and you're off on a brand new adventure.

So, me and Angel hitched a ride in a truck all the way across the country to the Michigan Womyn's Music Festival. We arrived just as all the lesbians were setting up camp, and what a sight that was, let me tell you. Girls, girls, girls, as far as the eye could see, in all shapes, colors and sizes. Angel let out a whoop of delight and stripped right down to her birthday suit, grooving and a-shaking to the rhythm of the conga drums that was drifting over from the Womyn of Color tent through the trees. Well, that was the last I ever saw of her, for my Angel was not too concerned with earthly possessions. I lay there on the ground all through the day when the hot sun practically singed my fabric, into the chilly evening when I almost froze to death. I don't mean to complain though. I'm usually pretty strong, a regular sock of

Gibraltor, but when it began to rain, and continued to rain for the next four days straight, even I began to lose hope. I lay there, watching those wild women paint their bodies with mud and chant a prayer to the Goddess for a little sun. It didn't work, but they had a great time, let me tell you.

Well, the festival ended and I thought I'd have to spend the rest of my days deep in the Michigan mud, but just when you lose faith, something always happens. I was picked up by Copperdaughter, washed out in the lake and dried off in the sun. Then she packed me up and off we roared on her motorcycle to Oregon, where Copperdaughter lived on women's land in a communal fashion. The women there subscribed to the philosophy of what's yours is mine and what's mine is everyone's. All their clothes were kept in one huge heap, and I never knew from one day to the next what I'd be doing; going out to the garden with Clover to pick an organic lunch; working down in the basement with Claylady throwing pots or with Copperdaughter soldering bracelets; mending the barns with Joist; or going into town with Moonbeam to work in a local copyshop.

Now, this working in town was a new development, and not everyone approved of what Moonbeam was doing, but to tell you the truth, the collective needed the money. There were many long talks about the subject: Clover wanted Moonbeam to find a job in a women-owned business, but those were few and far between. Claylady wondered if Moonbeam could convince her boss to let her wait on women customers only. Copperdaughter suggested Moonbeam take a shower in the outside stall they had recently put up, to cleanse herself of the male energy she picked up in town. They went on and on about it, until Moonbeam finally threw a fit and pointed out that for all their bitching and moaning, they were only all too willing to accept her hard-earned money that was no doubt tainted with male energy, for surely those dollar bills had passed through men's hands at some point in their lives, so how come no one had a problem with that? Joist said that was different, but it was too late. Moonbeam, who on the spot changed her name back to Monica, was already packing up a few choice items (including yours truly). We sped away in Monica's

Volvo and headed down the coast to San Francisco hungry for some city life, some diversity and some new and exciting fashion statements.

Well, in no time at all Monica found work in a copy shop in the Castro, and we settled into a nice little apartment on Seventeenth Street. We had some good times in that city, let me tell you. I saw things I never even dreamed of; dykes with nose rings, green hair and tattoos; lipstick lesbians in fishnet stockings and heels; gay men galore in tight 501's and black muscle-T's. Monica just drank everything in with her big brown eyes. She started writing in a journal to keep track of it all. Every day after work she'd curl up with a cup of mint tea and me warming up her feet, to write away the day's events in a black and white composition notebook. It was nice, just the two of us like that. I felt my life was finally settling down again. Sure, I was three-thousand miles from where I'd started, but hey, that s how it goes.

So, Monica got more and more into this writing thing and then she decided she wanted to be a poet. She started hanging out at City Lights, Mama Bears, Old Wives Tales and all the coffee shops and bars where they had open readings. Most of the stuff I heard I didn't understand at all, but, hey, what do you want? Like I told you, I'm only a pair of socks with very little education.

Then one night we went to the Artemis Café, where a famous poet from New York City was giving a reading. It was lust at first sight, let me tell you. As soon as Orca opened her mouth, I felt Monica's toes curl up right inside me and I knew something was about to happen.

After the reading, Monica went right up to Orca, bought all her books and asked her to sign them. She oh so casually mentioned that she wrote poetry, too. And then she sputtered all in one breath that she-had-really-really-really-enjoyed-the-reading-and-if-Orca-wanted-to-go-get-some-coffee-somewhere-that-would-be-great-and-if-Orca-ever-needed-a-place-to-stay-she-could-always-crash-on-Monica's-couch and then she blushed from head to toe (I could feel the heat, believe me), and took a deep breath. Orca smiled and said she'd love to, and if Orca spent more than five minutes on that couch, may the Goddess herself come down from the Queendom of Heaven and unravel my seams.

Orca stayed with Monica for two days before it was time to fly home to New York where unfortunately, her day job was waiting. Monica gave her a hug and a poem and then Orca asked if she had an extra pair of socks she could borrow; those airplanes are always so Goddess-damn cold.

I hesitated for about two seconds before I up and volunteered for the job. I was beginning to like the traveling life and I had never been to the city that never sleeps. What the hell, you only live once.

So we flew into Kennedy airport and managed to make our way home to Orca's sixth floor walk up on Second Avenue between Fifth and Sixth. Orca dozed off immediately, but I was too excited to sleep. Not to mention the noise; trucks roaring by, taxis honking, sirens shrieking, the toilet in the next apartment flushing... In time I got used to it, but that first night I was wide awake, on guard, ready for anything. I didn't see much though, except for a few roaches and they didn't scare me one bit. The only creature who really gives me the willies are kittens. I could tell you about a cousin of mine who got stuffed with catnip and practically ripped to shreds, but that's another story.

Well anyway, Orca was up at seven the next morning and ready to go by eight. She'd put on a white blouse, navy skirt, stockings, little earrings and a string of pearls around her neck. I went on over her stockings and then on top of me went a pair of jogging shoes. Orca hit the street and headed for the subway at Astor Place with her blue pumps in a plastic bag. There were hundreds of women on the train dressed just like her. Except that Orca wore a button on her collar that said DYKE IN DRAG which got her a few sleepy smiles on the number six line.

So I didn't really get to see much of New York. I was either on the subway or stashed in the bottom drawer of Orca's desk, with her sneakers, her pocketbook and a box of organic poptarts to get her through the day. It was back to the regular bump and grind. Orca still wrote her poetry of course, but less and less of it, as survival in the city took all her energy and then some. I was pretty beat too, My complexion was turning a sooty shade of grey and I didn't like that one bit.

But luck was with us. One day in early May a letter arrived congratulating Orca. She had been awarded a summer scholarship to a writers' colony in the Berkshires. They would give her a cabin, three meals a day, and even a small stipend. All she had to do was write. It was a dream come true!

Orca was ecstatic. She gave notice at her job, sublet her apartment, and off to the country we went. The dew was sweet against my fabric when we went for our daily morning walk. Then Orca wrote all day, stopping only to nibble on the lunch that was left right outside her cabin door. In the evening she'd go to the main house where a fire was lit, and cavort with the other poets.

The three months passed all too quickly, and soon it was time for Orca to head home. The fresh air had soothed her spirit and she wasn't happy about returning to the city. But what could she do? Maybe something would happen. We got in the car and started driving east. Around dinnertime we stopped in a tiny little town. After Orca ate we took a stroll to stretch our bones and lo and behold, we bumped into a women's bookstore. Orca was thrilled. She scanned the shelves to make sure they carried her books, and then stepped over to the bulletin board where a hot pink flyer announced a women's dance that very night.

Well, why not? Not only was Orca in no hurry to get home, but after three months in the mountains, she was hungry for a little action. We found the place and Orca started tapping her feet the minute we walked through the door. She wasted no time in asking someone to dance. I couldn't see a thing, as I was all bunched up inside Orca's cowgirl boots, but the woman must have been something, because they danced all night and I worked my fibers off soaking up that girl's sweat. Oh for the sock hops of yesteryear that my grandmother told me about, when a pair of cotton crews could get a little air!

Well, the last song was a slow one, and as we moved across the floor, Orca asked if she could escort her new friend home. The reply must have been affirmative, because we didn't even wait for the music to end before we were out of there. We entered an apartment and

Orca kicked off her boots and wrapped herself around the little lady who I could now see was none other than my long lost pal, Marsha, who always did have a weakness for those on the road artist types. Wow, was I excited! While Orca and Marsha was busy making music together, I rolled under the bed where I had a little reunion with the pink bunny pajamas before catching some shut-eye myself. I was exhausted by the whole thing, let me tell you.

So, the next morning, Orca got dressed, but she had to ask Marsha if she could borrow a pair of socks because I was laying low, believe you me. Marsha lent her a pair of yellow knee highs on the condition that she bring them back ASAP. Then they hugged and kissed for a few hours before Orca left, promising to return within the week and give up city life forever.

As soon as I heard the door slam, I rolled out from under the bed and Marsha scooped me up and dumped me into the laundry basket. So here I am, back where I started, clean as a whistle in Marsha's third drawer. If I were a philosopher or a poet, I would say something profound, like all's well that ends well, or it's a small world after all, or there's no place like home, or even love makes the world go round. But like I told you, I'm only a pair of socks, so I'll just say, it all comes out in the wash.

All In A Day's Work

"It's a miracle. You two girls came along just in time." Mr. Johnson looked us up and down as I silently corrected him: *not girls, women.* This is the year 2,001, I thought. Where the hell has he been?

"Both of you have been waitresses before?" he asked. *Waitpeople,* I thought, not waitresses, but again I said nothing and neither did Martha.

"Okay, you're hired." He reached over and removed his help wanted sign from the window. "We have a very simple menu here: Sunday brunch from eleven o'clock to three. If we do well, we'll start being open for dinner, too. Now remember, white blouses, black skirts, hair pulled back, easy on the make up. We're trying for an image here; we want to attract a professional crowd." He hesitated, looking us up and down again. "And one more thing. If any of those dykey-looking women come in here, you know, like the ones in that Gay Pride Parade last week, for God's sake, don't put them in the window seats."

"Yes, Mr. Johnson," Martha said, stepping backwards onto my right foot.

"Ouch!" I reached down to rub my toe.

"Be here an hour early to set up. See you girls tomorrow." Mr. Johnson turned his back and we were obviously dismissed.

"Sorry I had to step on your foot," Martha said, once we were out the door and safely out of Mr. Johnson's earshot. "But I could just hear the lecture about to burst out of your mouth. Listen, if you're going to be part of the Lesbian Police, you have to toughen up a little, sweetie. You hear all kinds of shit in this business, especially on the new

156

restaurant beat."

"I know," I said as we turned the corner onto our block. "But how do you stand it?"

"Never mind how I stand it. Let's figure out what we're going to do about it. We can't let him get away with that." Martha flopped down on our front lawn and I sat beside her.

"Well," I plucked a blade of grass and started tickling her bare leg with it. "We could wait until the restaurant was packed and then jump up onto the table right in the window and start making out wildly."

"That sounds like fun." Martha swiveled her body so she could put her head in my lap. "Do you think he'll draw a big crowd though? It's a new restaurant and most people have been going to Edna's for Sunday brunch for years." She closed her eyes to soak up some rays. It was a gloriously sunny day and I tilted my face up as well.

"I got it." Martha snapped her fingers and sat up. I should have known she was scheming as well as sunning. "We'll have to make a bunch of phone calls, though. There's my softball team, your writers' group, the over forty pot luck women..."

I was beginning to get the idea. "You think they'll all come out for Sunday brunch?"

"If we promise them service by the cutest waitdykes this side of the Mississippi? Sure." Martha grinned. "C'mon."

We went inside and started making phone calls. Martha called her therapist, her acupuncturist, her hairdresser and her accountant. I called our electrician, my bank teller, the piano tuner, the bookstore owners, the mail carrier and the woman who watches our cat when we're away. Everyone we called said they'd make some phone calls, too. Soon it was time for supper. After we ate, we each called all our ex-lovers. By the time I finished the last phone call, it was way past midnight.

"We better get some sleep," I said, rubbing my aching jaw. "Tomorrow's going to be a big day."

"Right." Martha let out a big yawn, stretched deliciously, and held out her hand to take me to bed.

The next morning we rose bright and early, and managed to get to the restaurant at exactly ten o'clock. "You girls look very nice," Mr. Johnson said, and I had to admit it was true. We had really femmed it up for the occasion: my black miniskirt was real short and tight and Martha's had a slit running up one side.

We started folding napkins, polishing silverware and filling salt shakers, and before I could say *quiche* it was ten-to-eleven. I glanced out the plate glass window and saw a long line forming halfway around the block. "Look at that," I said to Mr. Johnson, pointing with the glass I was wiping.

He looked out the window and almost dropped the stack of menus he was holding. "I don't believe it," he said, his lips curving into a huge, greedy grin. "And they said a new restaurant didn't have a chance in this town. Girls, let's open the place up. We don't want to keep our customers waiting." He took his post by the door, all ready to greet the public, a big smile on his face, the menus tucked under his arm.

"My pleasure." I stepped past him and opened the door with a grand gesture. Mr. Johnson's face froze as the restaurant filled with women. Martha's softball team filed by in full uniform, complete with bats, balls and gloves. Some Dykes on Bikes strode in wearing leather jackets, their helmets dangling from their arms, followed by a bunch of karate dykes in white uniforms, their blue, green purple, brown and black belts cinched at their hips.

Country dykes came in flannel shirts and workboots; city dykes came in make up and heels. Soon we ran out of tables and the butches stood in line patiently, fingering the loose change in their pockets and the femmes stood next to them impatiently, holding onto the straps of their pocketbooks and shifting their weight from side to side. Martha and I solved the problem by seating women on each other's laps, especially at the table right by the window.

Mr. Johnson, who seemed to be in a daze from all this, looked like he was thawing out a little when a well-dressed het-looking couple sauntered in, the man in a suit, the woman in heels and a skirt. "Good morning. Welcome." Mr. Johnson practically tripped over his own two feet in his rush to accommodate them.

"Good morning yourself, handsome," the woman said in a deep voice, pulling gently on his tie. I thought Mr. Johnson would faint as he realized he was talking to a drag queen, but I couldn't rush to his aid with smelling salts; I was too busy pouring coffee and serving blueberry pancakes. Blueberry short stacks was the house special, and I tell you I finally figured out where the expression, "going like hotcakes" came from, because these women ate like there was no tomorrow. I was so busy saying hello to everyone (I hadn't seem some of those dykes in years) and keeping them fed, that before I could turn around and say, "Oh, my aching feet," it was three o'clock and everyone was gone.

I flopped into a chair, totally exhausted, and Martha did the same. She had a drop of maple syrup on her right sleeve.

"Well at least those kind of people eat a lot," Mr. Johnson said. His tie was askew and his shirt was coming untucked from his pants, but other than that he looked no worse for the wear. "Let's count the money, girls."

Martha and I looked at each other. I cleared my throat. "Money? What money?" I asked, all innocence. "Martha, did you collect any money?"

She batted her eyes. "Why no. Mr. J. didn't say anything about money."

"You see, we assumed you'd have the good business sense to serve everything on the house on opening day," I said. "That way, all those customers are sure to come back. And you do want them to come back, don't you, Mr. Johnson?" Mr. Johnson furrowed his eyebrows, like he was trying to sort all this out. All of a sudden he got it. "Why, you…" He started coming toward us and I was up on my feet in a flash.

"Hold it right there." I reached into my back pocket, snapped open my wallet and pulled out my badge. "Lesbian Police."

"What?" Now Mr. Johnson looked totally confused. He stared at my upside-down pink triangle. "That's not a police badge."

"LESBIAN Police. Restrain him, Martha." I tossed her a pair of handcuffs I'd found under a table. One of the S/M dykes must have dropped them by mistake.

"Now, Mr. Johnson," I said, pacing back and forth in my best Cagney imitation. "Did you or did you not say, on May 5th, in the year two-thousand-and-one, that we should not seat any, and I quote, *dykey looking women* in the front of this restaurant?"

"Yes, but I..."

"Just answer the questions, Mr. Johnson." I took some notes on my order pad. "Thanks to all the hard work we did in the gay nineties, homophobia is now a felony, Section 269 Code L: criminals are to be tried by Lesbians and prosecuted to the fullest extent of the law." I thought for a minute, trying to come up with a punishment that would fit the crime.

"All right, Mr. Johnson. You are free to go until your trial. But, as Lesbian Officers, we are hereby revoking your restaurant license. This building is to be turned over to the Lesbian Community and used as a Lesbian Center to Promote Lesbian Culture and Pride. You are no longer welcome in this establishment."

"But, but..."

"Sorry, Mr. J., it's the law." Martha escorted him out and locked the door behind him, since the cook and the dishwasher had already made a run for it.

"We did it! We did it!" Martha ran back toward me and threw herself into my arms.

"Another victory for the Lesbian Police!" I kissed her and then sank back into a chair. "I never knew waiting tables was so exhausting."

"I'll say." Martha slipped off my black flats and started rubbing my feet. "I certainly have a new respect for waitpeople. It's all in a day's work, though. Anything to stop homophobia. You did great."

"Thanks." I leaned my head against the back of my chair and then quickly sat up as a series of short piercing tones shot through the room. "What's that?"

"I'm on call." Martha went behind the counter where we had stashed our stuff and pulled a walkie-talkie out of her shoulder bag. "Yes?" She pulled up the antenna and spoke into it.

"Lesbian Officer #157 here, standing in line at the Green Street Food Mart." I heard a voice coming through the static. "Two boys behind me reading *The Enquirer* and making nasty comments about Chastity Bono."

"We'll be right there. Can you stall them?"

"I pulled the tags off all my groceries. The cashier is running price checks. Over."

"Let's go." Martha handed me my shoes, put away her walkie-talkie, pinched my mini-skirted bottom, and the Lesbian Police were off and running again.

Two In One Day

"Ma, I'm going over to Julie's and then we're walking to Bennett's," I call into the living room. "I'll be back by six."

"Okay," my mother calls back. Sometimes I think I could yell, "Ma, I'm going out to commit pre-meditated murder, and I'll be home for supper," and she'd yell back, "Fine." My mother doesn't pay much attention to me. As long as I don't interrupt her soaps, and show up for my daily dole of Mrs. Paul's Fish Sticks or Morton's Chicken Pot Pie at six o'clock sharp, we get along just fine.

I cut through our back yard and walk through Julie's yard, which is attached to ours, separated only by a row of pine trees, like the dotted line Mrs. Cohen draws across the blackboard in algebra class. Mrs. Pellegrinni opens the screen door before I even knock.

"Hi ya, Wendy. C'mon in." She wipes her hands on her apron. One piece of hair droops over her forehead and she bends her neck to brush it aside with her upper arm. "I'm just making noodles. Sit down. Julie Ann," Mrs. Pellegrinni calls up the steps, "Wendy's here."

"Be right there." Julie's disembodied voice drifts down to the kitchen.

"Sit down, Wendy," Mrs. Pellegrinni repeats. "How do you like this Indian summer? Want a cold drink?"

"No thanks." I sit and survey the kitchen. Julie's mother has fresh home-made lasagne noodles laid out all over the house to dry, like wet laundry; across the kitchen counter, over the backs of chairs, draped across the piano bench in the living room. A huge vat of tomato sauce is bubbling on the stove.

"Hi, Wen." Julie bounds down the stairs in cut-offs and a halter top. Julie is curvy, as opposed to lumpy, like yours truly. I would rather die then go anywhere with my belly showing, but Julie looks like a million bucks. And I don't mean all green and wrinkly, either.

"We're going to Bennett's, Ma," Julie says.

"All right. Have fun."

We go out the front door and get about twenty feet before we hear, "Julie Ann," and turn to see Mrs. Pellegrinni standing in the front yard waving her change purse.

"What?"

"Get me a loaf of rye bread, willya? Tell them to slice it thin. Here." Mrs. Pellegrinni walks toward us, fishing a few bills out of her purse. "And get yourselves some Italian ices. It's hot."

Mrs. Pellegrinni goes back into the house and Julie stuffs the bills into her pocket. We walk up the block to the end of the development and turn onto the highway toward the shopping center in the middle of town. The shopping center consists of a pizza parlor, a kosher butcher, a Jewish bakery, a Chinese take-out, and Bennett's, a cheap department store and our daily after school destination.

"So, what was the movie last night?" I ask Julie, keeping my eyes downcast to avoid getting chewing gum, broken glass or worst of all, dog doo on my new loafers as we trudge along the roadside.

"Oh, it was really good. It was called *Where The Boys Are*. Did you see it?"

I shake my head. My mother never lets me stay up to watch the Monday night movie. Or the Tuesday, Wednesday, Thursday, Friday, Saturday or Sunday night movie either. So Julie always fills me in. "What was it about?"

"It's about these four girls who go to Florida for their winter vacation?" Julie ends all her sentences with her voice going up like a question. She thinks it sounds sophisticated. I think it sounds weird. "And they meet all these guys there, like one named TV, who's really wacky, and a really rich guy with a yacht, and a musician?" Julie pauses as a guy in a black pickup drives by and honks real loud, making us both jump. "And then there's this one girl, Melanie, she's really pretty? And

Wen, she has sex with two guys."

I look at Julie. "At the same time?"

She laughs. "No, of course not."

"Well, what do you mean?"

Julie grabs my arm and steers me clear of a plop of poop. "Well, first she does it with one guy."

"Did you see them do it?"

"No, what are you nuts? Gross." Julie wrinkles up her nose. "You just see her after her date and she looks a little messed up, and she kisses the guy, you know, and she says, don't tell? So you know they did it."

"So then what happens?" I bend down to pick up what looks like a dime but turns out to be a button.

"Well then," Julie grabs my arm again to make sure I'm paying attention. We stop walking. "Then she calls the guy to meet him for another date and he can't make it so he sends this other guy? And she doesn't want to go with him but he makes her. And then you see her crying in a motel room and calling her friend. Wendy, it was awful."

"Sounds it." We start walking again, both quiet. "Hey, look." I point to a white truck stopped at the side of the road. It says Stan's Cleaning Service on it in blue letters and the back of the truck is covered with black soot. It looks like it could use a good cleaning itself.

"Maybe he's got a flat," Julie says. Still, we swing a wide arc around the truck, both of us being well trained by our mothers not to talk to strangers, especially men in cars. But of course we turn our heads to look as a guy steps down from the driver's seat. He's wearing a blue mechanics uniform with his name stitched over his front pocket: HENRY. I don't know why, but after I read his name, I look down to his fly and my worst suspicions are confirmed: not only is his zipper down, but IT is sticking out. And if that isn't bad enough, he sees me see IT and he takes it in his hand and holds it out to me.

"Want to play with it, baby?" he asks, and that's more than enough to send me and Julie flying to the end of the highway, down the hill and through the shopping center's parking lot at full speed, not stopping until we collapse on the bench right outside Bennett's front door.

"Did you see it?"

"Oh my God, it was gigantic."

"And ugly."

"Gross me out!" We collapse in a fit of giggles.

"What did he say to you?" Julie asks, her eyes wide.

"He said, 'Want to play with it, baby?'"

"Oh my God." We break into hysterics again. Julie slaps my knee. "Play with it? That is so gross."

"Tell me about it." I roll my eyes. "Do women really put that inside them?"

"Wendy, stop!" Julie shrieks. "That's disgusting."

"I'm never having sex," I vow.

"Me neither." Julie agrees. "Can you believe our mothers do it?"

"Not my mother," I say. "I'd put a million bucks on it."

"How do you think you got here," Julie asks, "immaculate conception?"

She has me there. My mother is no Madonna and my name is certainly not Jesus Christ. "Well," I say, hugging my knees to my chest. "I know. She tried it once, but it was so gross she never did it again. That's why I'm an only child."

"Well, my mother did it three times," Julie says, referring to the obvious results: herself, her brother David, and her sister Nicole. "But I'm never doing it."

"Me neither. C'mon, let's see if anyone's here." We go into Bennett's and wander over to the pinball machines, where the other kids from our class usually hang out. But no one's around today. So we walk up and down the aisles, looking at things. It's only the middle of September but still all the Halloween stuff is out: Spiderman masks, plastic orange pumpkins, bags of candy corn.

"Hey," Julie says, "I gotta get a birthday present for Emily, the kid I babysit for? Let's go look at the toys."

"Okay." We go over to the toys and game section and start looking at dolls. Then a man in a business suit comes into the aisle, picks up a Thumbellina and starts talking to her. I nudge Julie with my elbow and point my head slightly in the man's direction. We can't make out quite what he's saying, but he is definitely talking to the doll. He flips her over and then turns slightly toward us to put her back on the shelf. I lower my eyes to avoid his. But guess what, this guy's fly is down, too! First I see the white cloth of his underwear, and then he moves and I can see the pink color of his flesh. Two in one day! I can't believe it.

"C'mon," I whisper to Julie, and lead her up the next aisle, stopping in front of The Game Of Life. "That guy looking at the dolls," I say to Julie, still whispering. "He's losing altitude."

"You're kidding." Julie walks to the end of our aisle and goes back to the dolls, pretending great interest in a Barbie flight attendant outfit. A minute later she comes back.

"Wendy, you think we should tell him?"

"Tell him?" I look at Julie. "Don't you think he knows?"

"I don't know."

"Well, he can probably feel the draft." I shrug my shoulders and peer down the aisle again. Now he's looking at a Chatty Cathy.

"C'mon, let's get out of here."

We walk to the front of the store and get some Italian ices; Julie gets cherry and I get chocolate. We don't talk about it, but we walk home through the curvy streets of the development instead of along the highway, even though it takes about half an hour longer. It isn't until we're right outside Julie's front door that we realize we've forgotten the rye bread for Mrs. Pellegrinni. And my mother gives me hell for being so late and I have to eat my Kraft Macaroni and Cheese at the kitchen table all by myself, ice cold.

Every Woman's Dream
to Deliah, with thanks

It was Friday afternoon. It was hot. It was muggy. All I wanted out of life was to be off this steamy street inside my nice cool apartment, drinking a tall, ice-cold glass of anything. Unfortunately my apartment was still a good six blocks away and I had neither wheels nor wings to take me there.

So I kept walking, and despite the heat even broke out into a run when the WALK sign on Amber Avenue changed into a blinking DON'T WALK. As I leapt up onto the curb, I heard a voice behind me, a male voice naturally. "Ooh, Mama, you should run more often," was his uncalled for, unappreciated comment.

I ignored him and kept on walking, as they always say to do (whoever *they* are) but I felt my face growing redder with every step I took, and I knew it wasn't just from the heat. What the hell did he mean by that crack, I wondered. Did he want me to run more often so he could admire my big beautiful breasts bouncing under my blouse in all their splendor and glory? Or did he think I should run more often to lose weight (I am wonderfully, gorgeously Rubenesque, and have no desire or intention to lose one precious ounce, thank you).

How should I know what he meant, and why should I care? Whatever his intent, it was, as my mother would say, not nice. I turned and started walking back toward him. I don't know why. Maybe because of the heat. Maybe because I had PMS. Maybe because this was only the nine-millionth-nine-hundredth-ninety-ninth time some jerk had made a crack about my body while I was just

167

minding my own business walking down the street. You'd think I'd be used to it by now, but I'm not. The audacity of the male animal never ceases to amaze me. Maybe it was just because, as my mother would also say, enough is enough.

I walked right up to the guy, all ready to lay into him about keeping his stupid misogynist comments to himself. I stood firm, my two feet planted on the ground, my hands on my hips, and stared. He was sitting on the bottom step of his stoop, bent over at the waist, trying to pour some Elmer's glue into an anthill. That's the kind of guy he was. Obviously any attempts at rehabilitation on my part would be a major waste of time. I decided to save my breath, so I turned and headed for home, but not before I caught a final glimpse of him out of the corner of my eye. And then he had to say it: "You sure got a lot of fat in the can, huh, lady?"

Before I could stop myself, I whirled around, looked him right in the eye, pointed a finger and spat out the words: "It's gonna fall off in three days, buddy." Then I spun on my heels and took my big beautiful butt home.

The weekend passed all too quickly, and before I knew it, it was Monday morning again. Work was the usual, and five o'clock came none too soon. I gathered up my things and headed for home. As I approached Amber Avenue, the DON'T WALK sign started flashing. Rather than sprint across the street, my body froze. I'll wait for the next WALK sign, I thought, even though this is the longest light this side of the Mississippi. I let out a yawn, suddenly overcome with lethargy. And then, just as suddenly, I was overcome with rage. I'm not going to let some stupid jerk stop me from running across the street or anywhere else, I thought, as my fury propelled me to the other side of the road in record time. A guy in a blue pickup honked at me but I gave him the benefit of the doubt for after all, he did have the light and he didn't make any nasty comments, thank God.

I slowed down to a walk and against my better judgment, let my eyes travel to where Elmer, as I had dubbed him, had been sitting last Friday. He was standing on the top step of his stoop, leaning back against the railing of his porch. Our eyes met. He had seen the whole thing naturally, and he opened his mouth, to make a lewd comment, no doubt, when something fell out of his shorts. He looked down, and visibly paled.

I looked down, too. There it was on the top step, right next to the toe of his black high-top sneaker. It was pink and soft-looking, about an inch and a half long, two at the most. I stared at it. It couldn't be... but it was. There was no blood or anything. It had simply fallen off.

I looked at it for half a minute, then I looked up at him curiously. He didn't seem to be in any pain. Maybe you could stick it back on with Elmer's glue, I almost said out loud, but even I am not that cruel. He must have been in shock, for he just stood stock still, staring. "At least you should pick it up," I said softly, but he still didn't move. And then, right before our very eyes, an army of ants marched up the steps in single file, surrounded the disembodied member, and with great and admirable effort, hoisted it onto their shiny black backs and carried it off. And that was that.

Plotting With The Devil

On the same day the news broke about Bret Easton Ellis getting a three-hundred-thousand-dollar advance for *American Psycho*, the novel which according to very reliable sources contained more grotesque atrocities involving women, children and animals than one could possibly imagine, Elaine Berkowitz learned that her brilliant, funny, heart-wrenching lesbian novel had been turned down for the thirty-seventh time.

"Don't get discouraged, doll," Rita said to her over the phone. Rita was Elaine's agent. For the past three years, Elaine had paid her fifteen percent of her writing income. Unfortunately (for Rita anyway) fifteen percent of nothing was nothing. Elaine had never met Rita, but pictured her as pencil thin (on account of her meager earnings) with enormous horn-rimmed glasses. "Now don't get depressed," Rita repeated. "Your break will come."

"Bret Easton Ellis certainly got his," Elaine murmured, staring at the *New York Times Book Review* on her desk.

"That was some deal," Rita agreed. "Five-hundred-thousand-dollars."

"Five? I thought it was three."

"It was three, doll. Didn't you hear? Simon and Schuster canned it at the eleventh hour. Seems all the broads at the publishing house made a stink about it." Rita was no feminist.

"So then what happened?"

"Then Random House bought it out for another couple hundred thou."

"You're kidding." Elaine shook her head. "And he doesn't have to give back the first advance?"

"Not a penny."

"Why not?"

Rita chuckled. "Obviously he's got a good agent, doll. One who reads the fine print."

Elaine started pacing around her study. "So, let me get this straight. This guy got three-hundred-thousand dollars not to publish his book, and two-hundred-thousand more to publish it?"

"You got it, baby. And get this: the poor boy is crying censorship. Who knows, maybe he'll even sue S&S." Rita chuckled again. She just loved literary gossip. "Anyway, you know with all the controversy, it's going to be a best seller. And then a movie. The boy's got it made."

"I should be so lucky."

"It'll happen, honey. Keep your chins up. Stan at Penguin said your writing was outstanding."

Elaine stopped pacing. "So?"

"So, S.O.S. Same old story."

"Not marketable," Elaine said with Rita in unison.

"Shit."

"Listen, darling, don't give up. It's still at three other houses" (they had stopped giving exclusive readings a long time ago). "In the meantime, if you could work up a good horror story, or better yet, a murder mystery, it wouldn't kill you." Rita laughed at her own joke. "There's your title. I won't even charge you for it."

"Thanks, Rita. Call me if you hear anything else."

"I will. Bye."

Elaine hung up the phone and drifted over to her desk. What a way to start the day. Another rejection. And to make matters worse, her car hadn't passed inspection yesterday, so she had to drive around with a REJECT sticker stuck to her windshield. I might as well stick it on my forehead, Elaine thought as she turned on her typewriter. She inserted a blank piece of paper, but instead of typing a word, she typed a number: five-hundred-thousand, with a dollar sign in front of it. Five-hundred-thousand dollars. She couldn't imagine it. How many months of rent, therapy and typewriter ribbons would that keep me in, Elaine wondered. Well, first of all, I'd buy a house, second of all I'd buy a computer, and third of all, I wouldn't need therapy anymore. All I ever talk about is my fear of success anyway.

Elaine picked up the *Times Book Review*, and skimmed the article again. God, the guy was only twenty-six. I'm old enough to be his mother, Elaine thought bitterly and then was instantly horrified, because she had sworn up and down and sideways that no matter what happened, she would never become bitter. She'd known from the start that the life of a writer was a difficult one, but she wasn't in it for the money. She was in it for the pure pleasure of putting paragraphs on paper and then discovering, for example, the alliteration that magically appeared in the first part of this sentence.

But unfortunately pure pleasure didn't pay the rent, and Elaine was getting mildly hysterical. She was forty-six years old and this novel (her seventh) was the best thing she'd ever written. Everyone said so. The women in her writers group, the editors who read the whole thing through even though they knew by the second chapter they weren't going to take it, and Rita who kept assuring Elaine she'd break through any minute.

"Break down is more like it. Hmmm." Elaine typed the two phrases out and studied them. Elaine Berkowitz was in love with words. Often she got ideas for stories or poems just by playing with words: break through, break down, break out, break up, throw up, shut up, shut down.

Elaine turned off her typewriter. Shut down, that was exactly how she felt. I get nothing for a love story between two women, and this guy gets five-hundred-thousand dollars for a book about cutting up women? It isn't fair. Automatically Elaine's eyes traveled to the index card above her typewriter on which she had typed: EVERYTHING IS FAIR AND THERE ARE WONDERFUL SURPRISES. She had seen that on a poster at her dentist's office. "Yeah, right." Elaine was mad at the world today. "If everything was fair, someone would be giving me five-hundred-thousand dollars, too."

"Well, that can be arranged," said a voice out of nowhere.

"Oh yeah?" Elaine looked up, puzzled, but not too concerned, for after all she was a writer and thus quite used to hearing voices in her head. "Who said that?"

"Elaine Berkowitz, meet the devil himself."

"What?" Elaine saw a puff of smoke, a burst of fire, and then a tiny red devil appeared on top of her typewriter. He was kind of cute actually, like a red Pillsbury Dough Boy, with horns and a tail. That's an interesting image, Elaine thought. She reached out to turn on her typewriter, and a jolt of electricity shot up through her fingers.

"Ow!" Elaine drew back her hand. "Hey, what gives?"

"I give," the devil said, sitting down on the return key of Elaine's IBM Selectric. "I am here to grant you your wish. Just say the word and five-hundred-thousand dollars will be yours."

"Far out."

"There is one small condition, however." The devil crossed his legs and leaned one elbow on his knee.

Elaine nodded her head. "There always is."

"The money is yours," the devil continued, "if you promise never to write anything lesbian again. You can write romance novels, historical novels, murder mysteries, whatever you want, as long as there are no lesbians in your work."

"Are you kidding? Hey, did Rita put you up to this?" Elaine put her hands on her hips.

"I'm strictly my own agent," the devil said, and Elaine started, realizing the devil knew exactly who Rita was. She wondered what else he knew.

"Impossible," she said aloud. "I'm a lesbian. I write about lesbians. That's who I know best. That's who I love. Why, I'd rather never write again than write books with no lesbians in them."

"Deal." The devil beamed. "I knew you'd see it my way."

"But, but," Elaine sputtered. "That's censorship."

"Call it what you want." The devil shook his head. "You writers are such a fussy bunch. Always have to find the exact word for everything." He got up and practiced walking up and down the spacebar of Elaine's typewriter as if it were a tight rope. "Here's my final offer: I'll

give you five-hundred-thousand dollars to stop writing lesbian literature."

"In other words, stop writing altogether." Elaine's tone was flat.

"If you say so." The devil hopped off Elaine's spacebar and
perched on a ream of typing paper on her desk. "Listen, if it's so
important to you to see your name in print, just look it up in the
phone book."

Elaine grimaced. On her worst days she did look herself up in the
white pages but she wasn't about to tell the devil that. She suspected
he already knew. "But I don't know how to do anything else," Elaine
whined. "How will I live?"

"On your five-hundred-thousand dollars." The devil took out a
nail file and started shaping his claws. "Just think of it, Elaine. You can
quit your night job at the telephone marketing office and be a lady of
leisure." His beady little eyes gleamed. "You'll be able to buy that little house you've always wanted and not have to worry about the land-
lord raising your rent every year. You can buy yourself a nice little car
that will run all winter." He looked up at Elaine who refused to meet
his eyes. He certainly has my number, she thought. "You can invest
the rest and never have to worry about money again." The devil licked
his lips. "This could be your last chance. You're not getting any
younger, you know. C'mon, Elaine. What do you say?"

"What about taxes?" Elaine asked. Years of being a starving writer
had taught her to be practical.

"Ah, taxes." The devil thought for a minute. "All right, what the
hell, no pun intended. Double or nothing. A cool million." The devil
stood up and stretched. "That's my final offer. One million
smackeroos in exchange for the L-word."

"You mean in exchange for my writing altogether."

"That's up to you." The devil took a few steps, leaving tiny red
footprints on the white typing paper. "You can write all you want.
There's nobody stopping you. But, I'm warning you. One look
between two women, one glance, one touch, and your money will be
gone in a heartbeat."

"But I can't censor myself like that!" Elaine cried.

"You can if you want to be rich." The devil folded his arms. "That's my final offer for real. Take it or leave it."

"I'll think about it and get back to you," Elaine said, borrowing a useful phrase Rita had taught her.

"Until tomorrow then." The devil whirled around and was gone in a blaze of fire and smoke.

Elaine shook her head a few times, as if to clear it, inserted a fresh sheet of paper into her typewriter and turned it on, this time without incident. Now that would make a great story, she thought, starting to type. A writer who sells her soul to the devil for one million dollars. "There's only two problems," Elaine said out loud. "First of all, it's not the most original plot in the world. And second of all, everyone knows you're never supposed to make your main character a writer. Hmmm." She struck a few more keys. "A homophobic devil, though. That's an interesting concept." Elaine typed a few more sentences and then stopped. She turned her right hand over and rubbed her thumb along the pads of her fingers. They were covered with a fine gray dust. Soot. And all along the right margin of the page she had just typed on were tiny red footprints.

"Whoa, wait a minute," Elaine said out loud. Like most writers, she was in the habit of talking to herself. She put her index finger on one of the small footprints. It was still hot. And a faint odor of fire and brimstone still hung in the air. "I know it's important to use the senses in your writing," Elaine said, "but this is ridiculous." She frowned. "This can't be real," she continued. "I'm a Jew. I don't even believe in the devil."

As if on cue, Elaine's typewriter started typing on its own like a player piano. SURRENDER ELAINE was the message that appeared.

"Oh my God." Elaine was now convinced. "This isn't a story I'm making up. This is the real thing. I can be a millionaire by tomorrow. What'll I do?" She sighed deeply. "But to never write anything lesbian again? How could I live with myself? But one million dollars? How can I pass that up?" Elaine felt like someone was playing ping pong inside her head, batting the argument back and forth. "I'll use the money to start a lesbian publishing company." Elaine was always a good creative problem solver. "Then I won't be writing lesbian literature, I'll just be publishing it." And even though Elaine knew she could never really give up her writing only to publish the work of other women, she held that compromise fast in her mind in order to get some sleep.

Shut-eye didn't come easily, though. Elaine tossed and turned, going from dream to dream. First she was a contestant on *Let's Make A Deal*, dressed as a Bic pen with a blue cap on her head. Monty Hall stood beside her, only his name was Monty Python and instead of a tie, he had a huge snake draped around his neck. Elaine could see the devil behind Door Number One, sitting at a table, counting out an enormous stack of one-thousand dollar bills.

"And in the box our lovely Carol is bringing down the aisle," Monty said, one arm draped around Elaine's shoulder, "is a contract from Houghton Mifflin for a novel written by Elaine Berkowitz." The audience was going wild. "The door, the box, the door, the box..."

Elaine moaned and rolled into another dream. This time she was a bag lady, dressed in rags with a shmate on her head. She huddled in a doorway on Forty-second Street, next to a shopping cart full of her unpublished manuscripts. It was a bitterly cold day and the wind was fierce. Pages started to blow down the street and Elaine, weak as she was, ran after them. Hunger gnawed at her belly, and in an effort to appease it, Elaine bit into page one of her twenty-ninth novel which began, "She was a dark and stormy dyke." She chewed voraciously, thinking, *I am finally eating my own words.*

Elaine woke with a start and automatically reached for the notebook she always kept by the bed to record her dreams in. "No, wait." She stopped herself mid-sentence. "One million dollars. I've got to at least entertain the idea." Elaine put down her pen and let her dreams go, like a kite shaped like a dragon that broke from its string, or a bright red balloon that accidentally flew off a little girl's wrist, or...

"Stop it," Elaine said, sitting up in bed. "You don't have to think in images. You're not a writer anymore." Elaine walked into the bathroom and began to wash up. "You're going to join the millions of people who used to be writers. Now they're selling real estate. But you," she looked at her dripping reflection in the mirror, "you're going to be a millionaire. Now I know money can't buy happiness," Elaine mumbled with her mouth full of toothpaste. "But there sure are a lot of things it can buy." She dried her face. "Like matching towels, for instance," she said, hanging a blue towel next to a maroon one.

"And who knows," Elaine said, slipping an orange sweater over her head. "Maybe you'll think of something to write about that has nothing to do with being a dyke." She stopped and sat down on the bed, one pant leg up around her thigh, the other hanging off her body like an extra limb. "Like what?" she asked herself. "What else can I possibly write about?" Elaine would never admit this to anyone, but she had considered this option before, even without the help of the devil. She knew she was a good writer, good as half the people who got published any day, but her books had two strikes against them before they even reached the editor's desk, on account of their "unmarketable content."

"Just write one mystery," Rita would beg her. "One romance, doll, one bodice-ripper. You're loaded with talent; I know you can do it. Just get yourself published, and then I promise, you can write whatever you want."

And Elaine had tried, for one long lousy week, but nothing would come out of the pen. Her fingers froze on the typewriter keys. "I can't do it, Rita," she finally admitted. "I can't compromise my writing. My life, maybe; my politics, definitely, but not my writing." And that was that.

So Elaine knew it was all or nothing. She finished getting dressed and went into the kitchen for some breakfast. Scrambled eggs, toast, home fries and orange juice. Usually Elaine went right into her study, barely gulping a cup of coffee, but today she lingered over a second cup, reading the morning paper, something she never did before she began writing. She liked to have her mind fresh for her work, not cluttered with the world's most recent crises. But today Elaine took her time, reading not only the news, but the sports section, the funnies, the fashion page and Dear Abby as well.

At nine-thirty, an hour later than usual, Elaine strolled into her study. She sat down at her typewriter out of habit, and inserted a blank page, a page waiting to be filled with words. Elaine had wondered more than once if her writing was worth the trees that had to be killed to support it. Maybe I'll be a great environmentalist, Elaine thought. I suppose I could write a speech about saving the rain forest without using the L-word. She picked up a pen and tapped it against a note pad. Holding the pen was comforting, and Elaine immediately thought about her mother, the ex-chain smoker who could always be found with an unlit cigarette between her lips. Maybe writing isn't an art form at all, Elaine thought, holding onto the pen for dear life. Maybe it's just an addiction or a nasty habit.

Elaine got up from her desk and wandered over to her bookcase. "Well, if I can't write, I might as well read," she said, her eyes scanning the shelves. "I'm always saying I don't have enough time to read, anyway." She chose a new women's poetry anthology and sat down in a big cozy chair. Elaine began to read, and before she knew what she was doing, she was making notes to herself for future poems, inspired by the wonderful women's poetry she was reading, the lesbian poems in particular, of course.

"Oh hell, this isn't working," Elaine said, slamming the book shut. And at the mention of his humble abode, the devil himself appeared on the arm of Elaine's chair in a cloud of fire and smoke.

"Hey, watch it. I'm not made of money, you know." Elaine was not yet used to thinking like a millionaire. "You already got shmutz all over my typewriter which I can't afford to have cleaned. Don't burn any holes in the furniture."

"Don't you mean my typewriter?" the devil asked. "No use leaving around the instrument of temptation." He waved a miniature checkbook in the air. "Here it is, a check for a million dollars, made out to one Elaine Berkowitz."

"Who's going to cash a tiny check like that?" Elaine asked, studying his little body. The devil was a very interesting shade of red, like the polished nails of a dressed-to-kill femme in a miniskirt and heels, or lighter maybe, more like the blush that spreads across a woman's chest from nipple to nipple after she's made love, or...

"Stop it," Elaine said to herself. Still the devil waited. All right, he was as red as an apple or a cherry. Elaine winced at the triteness of her images and shook her head. "You see," she said. "You censor yourself and you come up with drek. The richness, the integrity of your life is gone. I just can't do it. No," she shook her head. "I'll have to give up writing altogether. You know," she said, now addressing the devil. "It may turn out to be a big relief. To go out for a walk and not see a setting. To meet someone and not be composing a character sketch in my head. To have a conversation with someone and really hear what they're saying, instead of thinking about syntax and dialogue. To read a book for pleasure, without noticing the author stuck in a double plot reversal." Suddenly Elaine realized how very tired she was.

"I knew you'd come around." The devil unrolled a scroll. "All you have to do is sign right here."

Elaine picked up the pen, and just as she did so, the phone rang.

"Let the machine get it," the devil said, laying the contract flat on Elaine's desk. "This is an important business deal we're putting to bed here."

Elaine perked up her ears. "I'm busy writing so I can't come to the phone right now," she heard herself say (she'd have to change her outgoing message) "but please leave your name and number and I'll call you back soon."

"Elaine baby, it's Rita. Give me a call, doll, today if you can."

Rita! Elaine froze. What did she want? There was no affectation to her voice, but then again, there never was. She could just be calling to say the novel had been turned down by yet another publisher, or she could be calling with the news Elaine had been waiting her whole life to hear. She lunged for the phone, but the devil beat her to it and stood on the ear piece with his hands on his hips.

"Please, couldn't I just call her back?" Elaine pleaded.

"You pick up the phone and it's good-bye, Charlie," the devil said, folding his tiny arms across his chest. "You pick up the pen, and it's hello, easy street."

Elaine hesitated. The phone, the pen, the phone, the pen, screamed the studio audience that had recently taken up residence inside her head. She shut her eyes tight for a minute, imagining the house in the country, the Porsche, and the great leather jacket one million dollars would buy. Then the images disappeared as quickly as a cute dyke turning a corner and disappearing forever. Elaine opened her eyes and swatted the devil off the telephone like a cat batting away a mouse.

"See you on the bread line," the devil chuckled as he vanished for the last time. Elaine barely noticed his departure as she pressed the button on her telephone that automatically speed-dialed Rita's number.

"Rita Marks, Literary Agent."

"Hi Rita, it's Elaine. "

"Hi kid. Listen, I just spoke to Mark at Doubleday. He loved it. He said the writing's wonderful, the dialogue's delightful, the characters are so real they could walk off the page. He said it's sad, it's funny, it's..."

Elaine's heart pounded in her chest. "So, what's the bottom line, Rita?"

"Darling, the bottom line is it isn't marketable. But he wants to see your next book. We're making progress here. So get cooking."

"I will. Thanks." Elaine hung up the phone and went right to her typewriter. D-E-V-I-L, she typed out. "Devil dogs, deviled eggs, deviled ham, devil's food cake. Devil with the blue dress on. The devil made me do it. Plotting with the devil. Hmmm, I like that." She took the page out of her typewriter and put a new one in, typing Plotting With The Devil at the top. Elaine knew she had a devil of a story to tell, with a lesbian main character, no doubt. She wasn't sure exactly what was going to happen, but her fingers began to fly across the typewriter keys in a race to find out.